FOR LOVE OF A PAGAN

In marrying the millionaire Greek ship-owner Paul Christos Tina could be supposed to have done very well for herself—especially considering he had only wanted her to be his pillow friend in the first place! Now he had given her not only marriage and position, but money and a beautiful home in Crete—and he assured her that she in her turn had given him everything he wanted. But Tina had *not* got everything she wanted—for meanwhile she had fallen truly in love with Paul, and the one thing he had not given her was—his love.

FOR LOVE OF A PAGAN

For Love of a Pagan

by
Anne Hampson

MAGNA PRINT BOOKS
Long Preston, North Yorkshire,
England.

British Library Cataloguing in Publication Data.

Hampson, Anne
   For love of a pagan.
   I. Title
   813'.54 (F)   PR6058.A5547

   ISBN 1-85057-223-2
   ISBN 1-85057-224-0 Pbk

First Published in Great Britain by Mills & Boon Ltd. 1978

Published in Large Print 1988 by arrangement with Harlequin
Enterprises B.V., Switzerland.

Printed and bound in Great Britain by
Redwood Burn Limited, Trowbridge, Wiltshire.

CHAPTER ONE

He had known her for just less than three weeks when he asked her to become his pillow-friend.

'I would make it worth your while,' he promised lightly. 'You'd have a villa in the sun, a car, and an ever-increasing bank balance.'

She looked at him—at the tall and cultured Greek whose dark austerity and alien accent had attracted her from the moment they were introduced at an Embassy function she had attended in Athens, where she was staying as the guest of her aunt and uncle who were in the hotel business there.

'You're very quiet, Tina.' Paul Christos's voice brought Tina's thoughts back from that first moment when, looking up into the olive-skinned face of the man whose hand was gripping hers, her heart had given an involuntary leap and the blood seemed to have quickened in her veins. 'Does my proposal require so much considering?'

Faintly she smiled, shaking her fair head at

the same time.

'Not at all,' she replied calmly. 'I wouldn't waste my time on giving it one second's consideration.'

Paul was amused but by no means disconcerted. Tina felt it would be impossible to disconcert a man so self-assured as Paul Christos, ship-owner and producer of the finest olives grown in the whole of Greece. He was a millionaire several times over, her uncle had said. He had a luxury flat in Athens and a fantastic villa on the island of Crete, but he came originally from Langadia, in Central Macedonia, where a semi-pagan religion still survived in the ancient Dionysian worship which was uniquely combined with the worship of St Helen and her son St Konstantine whose sacred ikons had been brought from Thrace and were now kept in the sacred grove or *hagiasmata*. The cultists who indulged in this pagan worship were called 'Anastenarides'. They originated from Asia Minor, bringing their ecstatic religion with them.

Tina had little difficulty in associating Paul Christos with these pagans, since his features were etched on dark satanic lines, his mouth being harsh yet oddly sensual, his jaw inflexible, his eyes metal-hard, his hair raven black and forming a very pronounced widow's peak in the centre of a wide forehead, lined and subtly formidable. Strangely, though, she was drawn to the man, drawn in a way she had never before experienced. He possessed an indefinable power, a magnetism that was as exciting to her as it was frightening. Asking herself for an explanation of her feelings, she could only think that because he was so vastly different from any man she had ever known before, Paul Christos intrigued her, catching and holding her imagination. His wealth, for one thing, seemed unreal to a girl who had always worked for a living, having lost her parents early in life and having been brought up by the aunt and uncle who were now living in Athens.

They had moved there three years ago, but as Tina at twenty had an excellent job with prospects she had decided to stay in England. The job later folded up when the firm came on hard times and she was now struggling to make ends meet. It had been a strain to save for the trip to Athens, as the job she had managed to get was only temporary and in addition it was only part-time. She was now out of work, but optimistic about getting another job on her return to England at the end of the month.

Paul was speaking, in his suave and alien voice, asking her—not without a hint of sardonic amusement—if she was trying to convince him that she was an old-fashioned girl, to which she answered, her beautiful violet eyes meeting his across the table at which they were sitting, on the verandah of her uncle's hotel overlooking Constitution Square.

'I have certain ideals which I'm trying to hold on to.'

'You won't be able to hold on to them,' returned Paul with conviction.

'Your Greek girls do,' she reminded him, picking up the glass of iced lemonade which the waiter had brought to her along with the *ouzo* which Paul had ordered for himself.

'They hold on to their chastity, but I wouldn't say that has anything to do with ideals.'

'Don't you think it's nice that they should hold on to their chastity?' she said.

Paul's eyes became sardonic.

'They do it from necessity, not idealism. If a Greek girl wants to get married then she has to avoid anything that would blacken her name.' He looked at her above the rim of his glass; she saw that amusement had mingled with the sardonic expression in his pewter-dark eyes. 'I daresay your aunt will have told you that the Greek girl has no chance of marriage if she is seen even speaking to a man alone.'

Faint contempt entered Tina's eyes. For while she herself wanted to go to her husband pure, and new to the delights of sexual love, she at the same time abhorred the customs of the East where the woman had to be over-protected in the way being spoken about by Paul.

'Greek men amaze me, Paul,' she said, frowning. 'They insist on marrying a virgin, but they have numerous pillow-friends before marriage.'

He laughed and nodded at the same time, agreeing with her about the pillow-friends, but adding that they mostly had pillow-friends after marriage as well as before.

'They do manage to find virgins, though,' he assured her finally.

She said nothing, allowing her eyes to wander to the rush and hurry going on in the Square below. Thousands of people scurrying about, like little ants not knowing where they were going. The policemen at the crossings, imperiously blowing their whistles if someone, either on foot or in a car, did something out of place. The crowd had to wait patiently until it was safe for them to cross; likewise the vehicles had to obey the rules. Nevertheless, it was still chaotic as seen from here, high above the Square.

'Are you going to be my pillow-friend?' asked Paul again.

'I'll keep my ideals,' said Tina, and the finality in her tone ought by rights to have been more than enough to have stayed any further attempts at persuasion, but on the contrary it acted as a challenge and as she read his expression Tina knew for sure that Paul had always got what he wanted where women were concerned, since he had all *they* wanted—looks and physique, wealth, and an especial gift of finesse in the art of lovemaking. It was not for nothing that the Greeks had earned the reputation of being the most amorous race in the world. Tina had experienced his kisses, his gentle methods of persuasion, and it did not take much imagination to guess what he would be like as a lover. She had resisted, because of her ideals. It was owing to these ideals that she could resist; they were more precious to her than any thrills of the moment. When she found her lover it would be for ever, not for the fleeting interlude of erotic escapism and sensational flaring of the emotions. Her man would respect her. She would never believe that a man who had a woman before marriage ever truly respected her. Yes, she was an old-fashioned girl...and proud of it! Scoff they might, her friends of both sexes, but she was immune to

14

that kind of ridicule.

'Beauty such as yours, Tina,' Paul was saying, 'is a gift which you should share; you can provide untold pleasure to a man—to me!' Vibrant now his voice, and the eyes were dark as those of Hades himself.

'If I am beautiful, as you say, then that beauty will give pleasure to a man one day, the man who becomes my husband. I'll save it for him alone.' She smiled then, a winning smile, but it was a little thin for all that. She had a feeling of disappointment, a sense of loss. She and Paul had been keeping company since that first day, three weeks ago, and now it was all over, brought to an end by the question which she had been perceptive enough to expect. She had come on a two-month visit; there was still a fortnight to go.

'Yes, it will give your husband pleasure, but before then—'

'I've given you my answer,' she broke in. 'You're wasting your time, Paul.'

'I never waste my time where women are concerned,' was his bland rejoinder. 'I want you, Tina, and I mean to have you.'

'You'd be edified by a conquest, no doubt. But you're too optimistic. I don't know what kind of women you've dealt with before, but I assure you I'm not like any of them.' There

15

was nothing antagonistic in her manner, and her eyes even smiled as they looked into his. 'I suppose this is the end? I've enjoyed being with you for this past three weeks; it was rather lonely for me before you and I met. I've another fortnight here, but maybe I'll go home before then. I've got to find myself a job, as you know.' Her eyes wandered to the Square again, sloping from the former Royal Palace like a terrace. It was filled with outdoor cafés— tables set beneath trees, and white-coated waiters moving about in their midst. Tina watched a bootblack, then a man leaning against a tree idly twirling his worry beads. From somewhere among the shops that border- ed three sides of the Square came the soulful strains of *bouzouki* music, so typically Greek, so sad with the pathos contained subtly within the melody.

'Don't be silly, Tina.' Paul was frowning at her rather in the way a father would frown at an errant daughter. 'The fact that you've no job to go back to ought to be sufficient excuse for your accepting my proposal.'

'I don't require an excuse for doing some- thing which I know is wrong. I just don't do it, and that's that.'

'How determined you are!' He gave a small exasperated sigh. 'What am I to do with you?'

She had to laugh.

'Forget me and look around for someone else—' She spread a hand. 'There are thousands of tourists in this city. You can have your pick.'

'It so happens that I want you,' was Paul's quiet response. 'It's a long time since I was drawn to a woman the way I am drawn to you.'

'Just a passing fancy. You'll forget me within a week—No, much less than that.'

He looked at her with an odd expression.

'And you,' he murmured ironically, 'will you forget me in less than a week?'

She shook her head.

'No,' she answered frankly, 'I couldn't forget you in less than a week. In fact, I shall always remember this holiday and be grateful for it. We've done such a lot in these three weeks, haven't we?'

If there was regret in her voice it was unintentional. She was philosophical about life in general, and situations in particular. Fate gave, and fate took away. To battle or protest was a useless drain on one's energies.

'Yes, indeed we have,' agreed Paul. 'And we shall do a lot more yet.'

'How confident you are!' she laughed. 'I'm not willing to be your pillow-friend, so you won't be wanting to take me around any more.' Her thoughts backswitched to the lovely

17

outings they'd had in his luxurious car. He had driven her to Delphi and they had stayed overnight in order that she should witness the incredible glory of sunset and sunrise. He had taken her to Mycenae, to Corinth and Cape Sounion—this latter several times, as they liked the beach and enjoyed the swimming. In the evenings Paul had taken her to dine at all the best hotels, and on occasions to the *cafenions* and *tavernas* in the Plaka. They had danced, walked, explored ruins such as the Acropolis of Athens and the Roman ruins as well. He had said they would go to Crete on his yacht, but Tina had been wary of a trip like that, expecting as she had the offer that he had made today. It was inevitable, since his desire for her was apparent in so many ways. Well, it was nice while it lasted, but now it was but a dream, a very pleasant one which she would recall over and over again no matter what other interests should come along in the future.

Paul suggested they walked along Venizelou Avenue to Omonia Square. He seemed at a loose end, the first time since they had begun going about together. Tina shook her head, feeling that he would rather be alone just at this time.

'I'm going to my room to have a nice quiet rest and a read,' she said.

'As you wish.' His voice was indifferent; it came as a shock, so great was the change. She felt a sudden prick of tears behind her eyes and knew an anger with herself because of it.

'Shall we say our goodbye now, and get it over with?' she asked quietly. Another shock was in store for her. He stared her straight in the eyes, his mouth tight, his features harsh in the brittle sun of a July afternoon. The metal-grey eyes were narrowed and inflexible. Tina caught her breath, thankful that she was in a place of safety and not alone with him in, say, a place like Delphi at midnight, as she had been only last week. Midnight and the enormous moon over Mount Parnassus! He had taken her in his arms and she had felt all the magic and mystery of the ancient gods and heroes who had frequented the sacred precincts.

'No, we shall not say goodbye! You're being absurd, Tina! Ideals,' he scoffed, flicking a long brown hand in a gesture of contempt. 'You're living out of your time and you know it! Aren't you a believer in the liberation of your sex?'

'Of course. What woman wouldn't be? On the other hand, I'm not a believer in abandoning one's beliefs just because of equality. In fact, my beliefs have no relation to equality. They're mine, and precious. I shall hold on to

19

them no matter what the temptation.'

'If I had you alone, and could be sure of no interruptions, I'd show you whether or not you could resist temptation.'

She coloured, in the most enchanting way. She really had a beauty all her own, with pure alabaster skin, apricot-bloomed by the sun since coming over to Greece; her lips were rosy and full, her nose small and perfectly-shaped. The high cheekbones spelled good breeding, the wide brow intelligence. Her hair was pale gold with tints that often resembled threads of silver when caught by the sun; her eyes were deep violet, limpid and soft, framed by long curling lashes, dark and thick. Her figure was slender as a nymph's, her hands well-shaped with almond-shaped nails which had a natural polish. She had always been sought after at the dances and parties she attended, but no man had ever found his way to her inner senses; no man until this dark Greek who came from a pagan country.

'If you'll excuse me, Paul?' She spoke into the long silence which had fallen between them. 'I'll go inside.'

'I asked you to walk with me.'

'You didn't really want to go.'

'Why won't you come to my flat? You came one or twice and then suddenly fought shy.'

She looked at him and smiled faintly.

'You know very well why I fought shy, as you term it. I wasn't taking any risks.'

His eyes were mocking.

'Afraid, eh? And yet you've just said you'd resist temptation at any price.'

'Temptation, yes. But in your flat I'd be at your mercy.'

'You think I'd use force?'

She nodded without hesitation.

'Yes, I do. You're a Greek, Paul, and the Greeks are an amorous race.'

'All men are amorous, when the opportunity occurs.'

'Well, I don't intend that the opportunity will occur for you—not with me, I mean.'

'We shall see.' A pause and then, 'I'll come for you this evening. We'll dine at the Grande Bretagne,' he finished imperiously. Tina agreed to go with him, not because she was intimidated but more simply because she wanted to go with him.

They dined and danced and then they went for a drive in the car. He stopped in a lonely place far away from the city and took her in his arms. His kisses were like heady wine, the touch of his hands on her throat and her shoulders like the caress of a sea breeze but far more tempting. She kept a firm grip on her emotions, determined to show him that he was not the conqueror he believed himself to be. He drew an exasperated breath after a while and withdrew his hands.

'You little iceberg,' he said softly. 'How I wish I had you at my mercy!'

Tina could not help pointing out that he practically had her at his mercy now, since they were nowhere near to any houses.

'I'm not afraid, though,' she added. 'I believe you'd be scared I'd make a scene—what I mean is, I'd get out of the car and run.'

'If I let you.' He switched on the interior light and studied her with candid interest. 'I don't know about *my* tempting *you*, I rather think it's the other way round.'

'I haven't tempted you, Paul,' she protested.

'Not deliberately. But you're damned tempting at this moment, even. You're so beautiful, Tina, and your body's so soft and supple to hold. I want to caress more of it...and to see more of it.'

She turned away, embarrassed.

'It's late,' she said. 'Please take me back to the hotel.'

'You're very trusting,' he said, a curious ring to his voice. 'I could take you miles away from the city and—er—take advantage of you.'

'You're not the person to do that,' she

returned, confidently. 'Your flat, and the luxury of a bed, yes. I'd not trust you then. But something sordid is not in your line, Paul.'

He gave a slight start at her perception.

'You amaze me,' he said.

'Take me back,' she requested again.

He pressed the starter and the car slid onto the road.

'I'm a fool,' he asserted. 'I want to take you and yet something stops me. Is it your innocence, I wonder?'

'More probably my ideals,' she returned, leaning back comfortably against the upholstery. 'Perhaps you have ideals too?'

'If so, I haven't noticed up till now,' he replied with a sort of amused candour.

'You've had lots of women?' Already she had judged his age at about thirty-five or six, and it had amazed her that he was not married. But her uncle had told her that he had a reputation for being totally uninterested in marriage even to have an heir. He had cousins who could inherit, he had been heard to say casually when the question of his marrying happened to crop up in the course of conversation. However, there was one woman in whom he appeared to have shown a particular interest at one time in his youth, but she had married someone else and gone out of his life. Tina's aunt had said that she'd heard a rumour that the woman, Dora Vassilou, was now a widow and living in Crete.

'I've had a few,' admitted Paul casually. 'They come and go, and neither of us has any regrets at the time.'

It was a wonder they all hadn't fallen in love with him, she thought. Aloud she said,

'And I was to have been another added to your list, another who would come and go.'

He was silent, and only the purr of the lovely limousine could be heard.

'I rather think,' he mused, 'that you would have lasted much longer than the others.'

'Thank you for the compliment!'

He laughed and her heart caught. He was far too attractive when he laughed like that!

'You appear to have been immune to my compliments up till now,' he stated with some amusement.

'Not really. I'm feminine enough to lap them up just like any other girl.'

'So honest. How many more virtues have you, my child? I sometimes fear I shall resort to marrying you in order to get what I want.'

Tina laughed, but shakily.

Marry...Would she say yes? They were so different; she was from the West and he from the East. Women in his part of the world were nothing but slaves, subservient to their men-folk. They obeyed without argument; they knew their place and meekly kept it. She slanted Paul a glance; his profile in the darkness of the car was set and satanic. The set of the mouth was harsh and severe. He would be the master—the autocrat who would command and his wife would know better than to argue, much less to disobey.

She said, injecting humour into her voice. 'What an opinion you have of yourself, Paul! What makes you so sure I'd marry you?'

'I have a feeling that you would, Tina—' He swerved to avoid a cyclist without lights. 'You're not totally indifferent to me, are you?'

She decided to ignore the question, and changed the subject. But once in her bedroom at the hotel, to which she went on saying good-night to her aunt and uncle, she asked herself the question and this time she could not very well avoid an answer.

But she had known that she was not totally indifferent to his attractions. No woman with any emotions at all could be indifferent to a man like Paul Christos. A small sigh escaped her; she crossed to the mirror and regarded herself from head to foot, seeing a slender wand of a girl in a flowing gown of peach-coloured nylon with lacy frills between the four tiers of the skirt. The bodice made a snug covering for firm, small breasts, its low neckline revealing the sloping curves of her shoulders and the beautiful lines of her throat. Her skin, smooth and sun-tinted, was enough to send any man crazy, Paul had said one evening when his long lean hands were caressing her.

Tina slid the zip fastener and let the dress fall to the floor. Dainty underwear like this would have sent him crazier still, she reflected as she began to discard it.

Marriage...To be made love to by a man with the experience of Paul Christos. She thought of all the women he must have had, thought too that there would be nothing he did not know, either about lovemaking or about the needs and desires of women. She blushed at the idea of a man having such intimate know-ledge of what would take her to the heights of heaven. There was no mystery left if he knew everything...no room for experiment. But then a man like Paul did not need to experiment—he had done plenty in the past, no doubt. Colour mounted even higher in Tina's cheeks. She could not drag her thoughts from what he had said about marrying her.

Had he seriously thought about such a step? It wasn't feasible that he would, not at his age and still a bachelor. Why should he change now, just because she had come along?

She washed her face and hands, slipped into a night-gown and got into bed, savouring the coolness of the white linen sheets, for the temperature in Athens that day had reached a hundred degrees.

The following morning she wakened to the sun streaming through her window. It was not yet six o'clock, but it might have been mid-day, so thick were the crowds down there, in the Square. The Greeks started work early, then stopped in the heat of the day to take a siesta. At four in the afternoon the shops and offices opened again until about seven. Tina's uncle said that the rest revitalised you and that you found you were ready for an active evening.'

Tina herself liked the idea, since she was always tired at lunch time, the heat being over-powering at this time of the year. She rested for no more than a couple of hours, though, as Paul was always eager to take her to one of the lovely beaches, where they would cool off in the clear blue waters, then have refreshments at a café under the palms. Glyphada was one of their favourite beaches. Lovely summer villas of rich businessmen lay snuggling beneath the pine trees. It had an air of sophistication,

27

with many luxurious restaurants specialising in seafood.

After breakfast, which she always had with her aunt and uncle, Tina waited in the hotel lounge for Paul to come for her. He was taking her to Marathon, then they would have lunch and spend the afternoon at Cape Sounion. She was keenly looking forward to it despite the conviction that there could be a little awkwardness after what happened yesterday afternoon. Last evening had passed better than Tina expected, though a little thread of coolness crept in when once again Paul asked her to be his pillow-friend.

He arrived promptly, his eyes roving her slender figure to take in with undisguised admiration the cool, leaf-green dress that suited her so well, the white collar and matching belt, the white sandals and matching beach-bag made of linen.

'You look adorable,' he whispered as, tucking his arm beneath hers, he escorted her to his car. She glanced back, to see her aunt at the window of the lounge. Her aunt had warned her to be careful; Paul Christos had a reputation, and he was, in her aunt's words, 'dangerously and devastatingly attractive'. Have a good time, her aunt had advised, but make sure of how far to go.

The car slid away, into the maze of traffic in the Square. Then they were leaving Athens through Vassilissis Sophias Avenue and soon the road to Marathon was signposted after leaving the road to the small town of Laurium to the right. They passed through regions of vineyards, and areas dotted with ancient tombs where excavations had brought to light many treasures which were now in the museum at Athens. The journey continued, with the road running alongside the eastern side of Mount Pentelicon, noted for its beautiful marble that was used for the lovely temples on the Acropolis at Athens. Paul pointed out the road leading to the Tumulus of Marathon, erected at the beginning of the fifth century B.C. as a tomb of the Athenians who fell in battle. Paul told her about the battle and she listened, fascinated, actually able to imagine more than ten thousand Persians and six thousand Athenians facing each other for several days without either side ready to attack, the Persians by the shores where their fleet was moored, the Athenians on the higher slopes.

'The Persians decided to attack at last,' Paul continued, his finely-toned, accented voice most attractive to his eager listener's ears. 'And at first it seemed that the Athenians were losing, but of course everyone knows the result of that famous battle. The invading army was defeated and many of the Persians were drowned when they retreated into the marshes. The Tumulus stands—or is supposed to stand—right in the centre of the battlefield.'

'Isn't it interesting? I think Greece has the most fascinating history of anywhere in the world.'

Her enthusiasm pleased him; she saw his lips curve in a smile and her heart was very light. Tomorrow did not matter even though tomorrow might be the day they would say goodbye. Today the sun was shining, the fertile plain through which they were passing was lush with vines and olives; there were many happy hours ahead before she and he said their goodnights. In Marathon village they had coffee at a café in a garden, at a table shaded by a huge carob tree. Paul's eyes seemed scarcely to leave Tina's face. She could not help wondering if marriage to her was in his mind, in spite of her conviction earlier that it was not possible that he could be thinking of marriage just because she happened to come along and he was so greatly attracted to her.

They left the café and strolled for over an hour; he took her hand in his, curling his strong lean fingers around hers; she thrilled to the pressure, to the contact of flesh with flesh, to the comfort which the secure grip seemed to give her. She knew now that she had never yet found any small degree of fulfilment, that her life, though pleasant, lacked that vital relationship which only love can bring.

Love...She had not asked herself if she cared. An analysis of her feelings for this aristocratic Greek had been avoided, shirked in fact. And even now she determinedly switched her thoughts and considered her position when she returned to England. Jobs were no longer there for the taking; it was becoming more and more difficult to get one simply because those who had them made sure they held on to them. Well, she was practical enough to know she would get some kind of a job if she determinedly went out of her way to find one.

'Penny for them, my child...' The murmuring tones of Paul's voice were like a caress. 'I can see that they are not very happy thoughts.' He paused, but when she did not speak his tone became imperious. 'Come, tell me what brings that frown to those beautiful eyes.'

She glanced sideways at him.

'I was thinking of home,' she answered truthfully, 'and the job I have to get.'

He drew an impatient breath which she had half expected he would.

'You're stupid,' he told her bluntly. 'Here

31

am I, offering you every luxury, every opportunity to build yourself up a nice fat bank
balance, and you talk about getting a job!'

She smiled, though a trifle wanly.

'You don't understand, Paul,' she said
gently. 'I hope to marry one day, and I couldn't
go to a man without confessing to what I'd
done—'

'Then you're a fool,' he broke in exasperat-
edly. 'What the eye doesn't see the heart
doesn't grieve over. In any case, what has it
to do with your future husband if you have enjoyed a love affair before marriage?'

She sighed with impatience and shook her
head.

'You only talk like that because it suits your
own ends for me to become your—your—
pillow-friend. If I were your sister you'd not
be adopting this attitude.'

She saw his mouth tighten; it shocked her
to see it so thin that it was frighteningly
ruthless. The man's veneer was attractive...but
what lay beneath its suave sociability?

'As I don't happen to have a sister,' he said
curtly at last, 'there is no point in talking about
it.'

'If you did have a sister?' she persisted,
watching his profile as he turned his head, looking straight before him to where a man in baggy

vraga was sitting astride a donkey, his wife trudging along just a few paces behind him. Tina frowned and withdrew her gaze; she did not like Paul's fixed and formidable expression any more than she liked the picture of that couple down there, the husband taking it easy on the animal's back while his wife, obviously fatigued by the broiling heat, dragged herself along. Through the filter of her own reactions Tina felt she could never become used to such sights...and she would have to become used to them if she were to accept Paul's offer, or even if she should—by some miracle—become his wife. Well, as neither was a possibility she dismissed the thought, but Paul's next words immediately brought it back again.

'If I had a sister she would remain chaste. However, we were talking about you, Tina, and this ridiculous obsession you have of going to your husband as lily-white as the day you were born. Forget your outdated scruples and take what life has to offer. I promise you, my dear, that I'll be a kind and generous lover.' He stopped, by the roadside just in the shade and privacy of some olive trees. Myrtle and erica caught the sunbeams, oleanders by a dry stream bed gleamed white, and away to the east spread the lush green vineyards. 'Kiss me,' commanded Paul, standing above her, towering

33

so that she was forced to tilt her head right back in order to meet his gaze, a gaze that was metal-dark, commanding, masterful.

Her heart jerked; her pulses were beating a shade too quickly. He ordered her again to kiss him and she found herself going up on tiptoe to obey him. But she was caught within the steel hawser of his arms, brought to his hard and virile body and as he bent his dark head she parted her lips, eagerly, sacrificially, yearning for his kiss. It was gentle, then possessive, then hurtfully passionate. 'You *will* become my pillow-friend!' he told her masterfully. 'I shall break down this absurd and profitless aversion you have!'

Tina shook her head...but for the first time she was afraid...afraid of herself and her desires, afraid of Paul and his attractions which, mingled with his mastery, presented something that could very well prove invincible.

CHAPTER TWO

Her decision was reached the following morning. She must curtail her holiday, must escape while there was still time. Last night, after the meal and dancing, Paul had taken her into the garden and used all his expertise to break down her resistance, and he had come very close to succeeding. His hands had caressed where they shouldn't have—had touched her breasts, her back below the end of the zip fastener which he had so deftly brought down without her even being aware of it. His kisses had made her swoon, firing her with longing, with the desperate urge to abandon all her ideals and allow him to make love to her. But somehow, strength had come to her and she fought him off, turning away, too embarrassed to do anything but run from him, without even saying goodnight. She had not turned her head, but she had his low laugh ringing in her ears even after she had reached her bedroom...his laugh of sheer triumph.

'Going?' echoed her aunt when at breakfast

time she had declared her intention of going home just as soon as she could get a flight. 'What's happened, love?'

Tina coloured, and knew that her aunt would instantly guess what had happened.

'It's Paul, Auntie Doris. I feel the time has come for me to put an end to our friendship.'

'I see...' Her aunt was frowning slightly. 'Well, I must admit I saw it coming. Paul has this reputation, I know. He thinks every woman he meets can be bought. He's not alone in that; all wealthy Greeks have this inflated ego. It's probably a legacy from the ancient times when Greece was the all-powerful in the known world—' She broke off and frowned. 'Here's your uncle to join us, so we can't talk.'

'It doesn't matter if he knows, Auntie. We've never had any secrets from one another.'

Her uncle sat down, a big man of fifty-eight years, grey-haired, blue-eyed and jovial for the most part but with the ability to be serious when the occasion required him to be so.

His wife was eating her toast; she glanced at Tina and then at her husband. She said at last.

'Tina wants to leave us—today if possible.'

He gaped, putting down the knife he had picked up.

'Leave us, girlie? What have we done to cause you to make a decision like that?'

She smiled affectionately and assured him that it was nothing he and her aunt had done. She then went on unhesitatingly to explain, blushing a little as she saw his eyes narrow perceptively.

'He didn't ask you to be his pillow-friend, though?' her uncle began, then nodded as her colour deepened.

'You didn't tell me that!' exclaimed her aunt angrily. 'Just wait until I see him! He'll get a piece of my mind—wealthy ship-owner or not!'

'You're afraid of yourself?'

'Yes, Uncle Frank, I am afraid of myself. Paul's far too attractive, just as Auntie said.'

'Are you in love with him?' her aunt wanted to know.

'Not madly,' answered Tina, surprised that she was able to inject a touch of humour into her voice. 'I'm escaping while I'm still able to.'

'Good girl! His kind are not for your kind, Tina. You have high ideals and it would be a shame if some damned Greek robbed you of them.'

'Now if it were marriage...' Aunt Doris was thoughtful, toying unconsciously with the butter on her plate. 'Would you...?'

'It isn't marriage he wants, Auntie, but even if it was I don't think I'd be interested. He's so different from me—his background, his

37

pagan ancestry—' Tina shrugged and changed the subject. 'Will you get the airport for me, Uncle, and see if there's a seat on any flight today?'

'I will if that's really what you want, love.' He shook his head regretfully. 'There's no need to go, you know; I can soon tell him to keep away from you.'

'He'd take no notice,' she said with conviction. 'Paul wants me and he'll continue to pester me until the moment I leave Greece.'

Her aunt was nodding. She was afraid for her niece; Tina knew her well enough to realise that. It would be better all round if she left, she said, looking from her aunt to her husband.

'Also,' she thought to add, 'I have to find a job, and the sooner I start looking the better.'

She got a flight that very morning and had left the hotel before the time arranged for her meeting with Paul. Last night she had made the arrangement before they went into the garden. The events later should by rights have cancelled out that arrangement, but she knew instinctively that Paul would keep the appointment and as she was leaving her aunt and uncle at the airport, to where they had brought her in their car, she glanced at the clock and wondered what Paul was thinking at this moment, as he would have learned from the desk clerk that she had left that morning for England.

'Goodbye, dear, Safe flight.'

A kiss for her aunt, a kiss and hug for her uncle and she was on her own, feeling lost and lonely and almost wishing she had not decided to accept her aunt's offer of a couple of months in Greece.

The flight home was uneventful; her thoughts were never for one moment free of the image of Paul and she often sighed and felt that the time would never come when she could look back and view the situation objectively, un-emotionally, and without regrets. Yet what would those regrets be? Would she ever have her ideals shattered to the extent whereby she would be sorry she had not taken advantage of Paul's offer? She knew that to many girls that offer would have been so alluring that it would have been irresistible.

The tiny flat looked shabby and cold as she entered it and stood looking around for a moment, her suitcases still in her hands. She shivered, and her thoughts naturally flew to Athens and the sun pouring down on the love-ly temples of the Acropolis, to the hotel which was so luxurious and yet possessing an air of cosiness one would not expect in so large and well-run an establishment. She thought of Paul, who would be thinking about her with anger, wishing he had arrived at the hotel earlier, when—so he would believe—he could have swayed her from her resolution to leave.

The searching for a job proved more disheartening than Tina had expected. She visited the Job Centre every day, perused every newspaper, even called in at shops and offices to see if there were any vacancies. At last she came to the conclusion that she would have to take a domestic post, as her money was running short, since she had to supplement from her meagre savings the money she received from the state.

One of her friends with whom she had worked before going to Greece called in one evening and stayed for supper. It was a beautiful sunny evening and they sat before the open window in Tina's little sitting-room. Bernice, dark-haired and brown-eyed, was, at twenty-four, engaged to a farm worker and her prospects were far from rosy. She would have a cottage on the farmlands, a long trek to the shops and a longer one to the train if she wanted to go into town. But she was madly in love and Tina envied her as she sat listening to her, eagerly listing all the things they had been buying for the house. The wedding was to be in August, just a month from now. Tina was to be the chief bridesmaid along with three others, friends of Bernice and her fiancé, David. Bernice knew that Tina had returned from Greece earlier than she had intended and she was naturally curious as to the reason. After a small hesitation Tina merely said,

'I thought I'd better come back and begin looking for work.'

'Jobs are hard, much harder than a few months ago.'

'I know it,' grimly from Tina. 'There just isn't anything except domestic work. It seems that servants in the house are still at a premium. Girls don't want that kind of drudgery these days. However, I am seriously thinking of taking on a job of that kind.'

Bernice frowned her disapproval.

'You can't, Tina! Besides, you have to live in, and what about this little place?'

Tina glanced around, finding nothing attractive in it any more.

'I wouldn't mind living in, not if I had my own rooms.'

'It's not advisable to give up your home,' said Bernice. 'You never know when you might want to come back to it.'

'I shall just have to take that chance. I wouldn't want to come back if I got a

41

comfortable job and nice accommodation.'

'There's nothing in a life like that,' protested Bernice. 'From what I know of these jobs you're tied, expected to be there in the evenings.'

Tina nodded in agreement.

'Some evenings, yes, but I expect I shall have some time off. Domestic work is certainly better these days than it used to be.'

Bernice said nothing, but she was troubled. And she was even more troubled when, having managed to get Tina on her own at the wedding, she learned that already Tina had accepted a post and was selling up most of the things in her flat.

'I wish you could have got the sort of job you wanted,' she said. 'You're unwise, Tina, to give up your little home.'

Tina was thoughtful. Her aunt and uncle had both expressed their desire to have her with them. They could find her a job in the hotel— there were always vacancies of one kind or another, her aunt had written, adding that she would like to see her niece as the receptionist at the hotel.

But to go to Greece, and especially to Athens, would only be courting trouble, since it would very soon come to Paul's ears that she was back there, and the persuasions would begin all over again.

Within a week after taking the post of housekeeper to Mrs France-Cobet Tina knew she had made a terrible mistake. At the interview the woman had been charming, had said that Tina would have an easy job with a good deal of free time. The suite shown to her was more than comfortable, it was luxurious. On her arrival, however, Tina was told that her employer had decided she would be more cosy in a room at the top of the house. It was small, with a roof light; the bathroom was not en-suite like the other but along a dark uncarpeted corridor. There was no sitting-room. As if this were not enough Tina was to discover that apart from a daily who came in twice a week no other help was kept in this three-storeyed, seven-bedroomed house. There was the cooking, washing, shopping, and in addition the woman and her husband did a good deal of entertaining.

When another week had gone by Tina thought it was time to complain, to come to some understanding about the accommodation and the time Tina was promised she would have off.

'Well,' said her employer vaguely, 'you can have time off during the day, if you've done your chores, that is. My husband isn't in for

43

lunch and as you know I'm on a diet and need only salads and cold meats and some fruit as a desert.'

'There's too much work for one,' Tina had pointed out perseveringly. 'I feel I've been cheated, since you made promises you haven't kept. My room, for instance—you showed me a suite—'

'Yes, but that was impulsive of me,' broke in the woman defensively. 'My husband was furiously angry that I'd promised you one of the guest suites. After all, you are only a servant.'

It was a fruitless effort on Tina's part and she decided that the only thing she could do was to look for somewhere else. But she remembered her friend's warning, her advice that it was foolish to give up her home. If only she had the flat now! She would have packed up on the instant and walked out.

She found herself brooding, and the inevitable result was that her thoughts would fly to Paul, and the offer he had made. Staunchly she resolved to hold on to the ideals she had kept for so long, yet it was natural that she should conjure up the vision of herself established in a villa in the sun, with a car and, as Paul had put it, a mounting bank balance. No work to do, pretty clothes to wear, mixing

44

with people like Paul...

The picture faded and a much more attractive one came into focus. She saw herself meeting the man she would marry, pictured herself falling madly in love, and being loved. There would be a lovely white wedding, and the purity which orange blossom represented—but which had now become a mockery. In her case, though, it would retain its meaning; her husband would know she had never indulged in an affair before her marriage.

But where, and how, was she to meet the man of her dreams? Both her leisure and her money were limited. There was suddenly no hope in her heart that the dreams would come true.

'We're entertaining on Friday, Tina...' Her employer's voice reached Tina while she was dusting the banisters and she looked down, to where the woman, clad in a glamorous negligé, was standing, a little pekinese snuffling at her moccasined feet. 'There'll be eight of us for dinner. We'll have pheasants, with that special stuffing—'

'It takes a long time to make,' broke in Tina, almost ready to walk out, regardless of the fact that she had nowhere to go. 'It's too much for one person, and then the waiting on—' She shook her head and added, 'I feel I ought to

45

leave you, Mrs France-Cobet.'

'Leave?' The woman blinked disbelievingly. 'You haven't given the job a fair trial, Tina!' she said tautly. 'It seems to me that servants don't want work these days—just the money and days off!'

'If you employed someone to help with the housework—' began Tina, but her employer interrupted to point out that she did employ a daily help. 'Yes, for two days a week,' said Tina shortly. 'It isn't enough. I don't know how you managed before I came, but I'd like to bet you had more than one person to look after this large establishment.

The woman reddened and turned away. Perceptively Tina guessd that whoever had been here had walked out. She later questioned the daily, and learned that there had been two housemaids and even they complained that the work was too much. They both walked out together and Mrs France-Cobet had to resort to temporary staff supplied by an agency.

Tina was cleaning the brass letter-box the following afternoon when a car slid with a grinding crunch on to the loose chippings of the forecourt. She glanced in through the hall, to see if her employer had heard the car approaching. Yes, she had, apparently, because she was coming from the drawing-room, the pekinese under one arm.

Tina, with the intention of making herself scarce, entered the hall, only to stop dead on hearing a voice that sent her mind blank almost to incredulity. She swung round, the colour ebbing from her cheeks, her hands, soiled from the metal polish, closing convulsively upon duster and tin.

'You!' The one word escaped from the bewildered confusion of her mind. She was stunned—too stunned even to ask herself why he was here.

'Good afternoon.' Mrs France-Cobet's voice was cold, but her gaze was one of deep interest. It was plain that the tall distinguished figure of the Greek had arrested her whole attention.

He made no attempt to answer. Tina saw that his eyes were narrowed, the light within them brittle. His mouth was compressed, his jaw taut and on his brow there was a deep furrow that was much more than a frown. He looked more formidable than Tina had ever seen him, and as his dark eyes moved slowly from Tina's face to that of her employer he seemed even more formidable—harshly, ruthlessly frightening, in fact.

'Get your things together, Tina.' His tone was soft, his eyes threatening as they returned to Tina's pallid face. 'Put that down.' His hand indicated the duster that was now dangling to the floor.

'My good man,' began Mrs France-Cobet haughtily, 'what does this intrusion mean? I do not allow my servants to have men visitors! Kindly remove yourself, and your car, from my property.'

Silence, so deadly that Tina's heart gave a plunge, so savage was Paul's expression now.

He said nothing to Mrs France-Cobet, however, but moved from the step into the hall and then, with firm and masterful deliberation, he took both duster and tin from Tina's fingers and tossed them down at her employer's feet. Staggered at the unexpected action, the woman just stared, speechlessly, her puffed and crimson cheeks the sure indication that fury had taken possession of her. Paul spoke, his voice a whiplash of authority.

'Go and get your belongings,' he ordered. 'I'll give you five minutes. If you are not down by then I shall come and find you—'

'How dare you!' Mrs France-Cobet found her voice at last. The dog was struggling in her arms and she put it down on the floor, then straightened up, to face the man who stood there, poised and erect, his air one of supreme authority, his glance one of contempt as it swept the woman's figure from the top of her head to her expensively-shod feet.

'I am here,' he informed her softly, 'to collect my wife.'

'Your—!' If the woman had been staggered before she was now stunned into silence as her eyes wandered from Paul's impeccably attired figure to that of Tina who was wearing a pink nylon overall, her hands dirty from the polish, her hair a little awry, with little damp tendrils clinging to her forehead.

'Tina!' Imperiously Paul spoke her name. 'Do as I tell you—at once!'

She began to shake her head but turned at the same time, and made her way to the staircase at the far end of the hall. Her mind was still chaotic, but she was conscious of a certain lethargy as well; it was easier to be managed— ordered was of course the more appropriate word—and she had no desire to put up a fight which she knew instinctively she would lose. Moreover, she saw Paul's appearance as a means of escape. He had said she was his wife, but she attached no particular importance to that. It was said merely to put Mrs France-Cobet in her place.

She was rather more than five minutes, because she had to wash her face and hands and change her clothes as well as pack, and collect the few books and ornaments which she had put out in a pathetic attempt to make the garret room more attractive. Paul was in the car when she came down. Her employer was nowhere about and Tina hesitated, reluctant to leave without saying goodbye. But Paul had slid from the car; Tina saw him through the long narrow side-window that adjoined the front door. So she opened the door and within seconds he had taken her suitcases and put them into the boot.

'Inside!' He thumbed to indicate the passenger seat, while with the other hand he dropped the lid of the boot. He reached her before she opened the door and he did it for her, glancing down for a fleeting moment before helping her in, with a hand beneath her elbow. As gallant as ever, she thought. She had loved his impeccable manners. Englishmen had forgotten these nice things that women lapped up—well, the young ones had. Only the older men remembered, and Tina had often wondered if they realised just what pleasure it gave their womenfolk when they performed these little services for them.

She had not spoken another word since the brief exclamation uttered on first seeing him—an apparition, she had thought for one incredulous moment. Now, she slanted him a glance as he got into the car and said, in a quiet but firmly determined voice,

'Thank you for rescuing me, Paul, but I'm not being your pillow-friend—'

'Shut up,' he commanded.

'I don't understand.' Her heart was pounding. Did he really want to marry her, after all?

'I don't expect you do.' Paul pressed the starter, slipped the gear-lever and the car left the gravel with the same sort of crunch as when it was brought to a standstill less than fifteen minutes before.

'How did you know where I was?'

'I went to your little flat—got the address from your aunt—'

'My aunt? She warned me about you, so I can't understand why she should give you my—'

'If you listen, without interrupting, you'll understand everything in less than two minutes.' Stern the quality of his voice, admonishing and curt. Tina found herself saying, 'I'm sorry,' and then waiting for him to explain.

He said, in that attractively accented voice, 'I want to marry you, Tina. That's the most important thing I have to say. And now, as to how I come to be here. I told both your aunt and uncle that I wanted you for my wife. Your aunt was hesitant, but in the end she said she felt it was her duty to give you the opportunity of hearing my proposal. When I arrived at your flat a young woman said you'd left—sold up—and gone into service, but she did not know where. However, she supplied me with the address of your friend, Bernice, who, I soon discovered, was exceedingly troubled by the fact that you had given up your home and gone into domestic service—' He stopped and as she glanced sideways at him Tina felt her nerves begin to quiver again. That he was blazing mad at the idea of her being a servant was more than plain and she felt that if it wasn't for the safety of the car she would be shaken mercilessly for lowering her dignity the way she had. 'Bernice was more than ready to give me your address. She wants to be maid of honour at our wedding, by the way.' Quiet now the voice, and tinged with humour.

'You—you w-want to marry me, then?'

'I thought I'd made that clear way back there, when I said I'd come to collect my wife.'

Tina said nothing. It was easier to sit and think, to sort out this situation in the mind alone rather than with the aid of words, which were an effort anyway. She felt that it was only desire which had impelled Paul to make the decision to marry her. Desire...She herself knew for sure that if she did become his wife, she would be madly in love with him within a week. Would she be happy to remain an unloved wife? Paul would be kind—at least so long as she obeyed his whims and kept to her woman's place, remembering she was in the East, where the man was supreme master whose every word was a law to be obeyed.

Kind...Was kindness sufficient? She frowned and suddenly had to break the silence.

'You seem very sure I will marry you, Paul.' She glanced through the window, staggered to realise that she had not asked him where they were going. She had been so relieved to get out of that house that she had not really cared where she was going.

'Of course, I'm sure.' He swung the car round a corner and put his foot down on the accelerator.

'Where are we going?' she asked, staring through the window again at the unfamiliar landscape.

'To a delightful little inn I have found called the White Hart. It's in Dorset and that's where we are going to spend our honeymoon.'

'But I haven't said I'll marry you!' There was more than a protest in her lovely voice; there was indignation and a plea, and a little catch that impressed him more than anything else.

'Don't be afraid, Tina,' he said gently. 'I do

realise that you have your back to the wall, as it were. You had written to Bernice telling her of the garret you were in, and the work you were expected to do. I knew without any doubt at all that you'd raise no objection to being rescued by me. I hold all the aces and I admit I intend to use them. I want you, Tina, but you have nothing to fear from me. I shall make you a good husband—'

'But you don't love me!' she broke in tremulously.

'I would not lie,' he said, 'and so I shall admit that it isn't love which impels me to want you for my wife.' He paused and she saw his profile become taut. 'Perhaps I am incapable of love—I don't know.' His mind drifted; she knew he was not with her and wondered if he were with that other girl, the one her aunt had mentioned and who was now widowed and living on Crete... the island where she would be living if she married Paul. 'Well,' he said at last, 'love isn't all that important. From what I have seen it doesn't last anyway. Respect does last, and I respect you, Tina, respect you greatly for those ideals you are so firmly holding on to.'

She said after a long silence,

'Is this hotel far away?'

'It'll take us another couple of hours to get there.'

'I expect it's very plush.'

'Not so you'll feel you have to dress like a princess.' He glanced at his watch. 'We shall be in time to get you some clothes in Dorchester. We have to drive through the town to get to our little inn.'

'I haven't said I'll marry you,' she murmured, 'so it isn't right for you to buy me clothes. I have some nice evening dresses with me—those I wore when I was on holiday.'

'I want to buy you something glamorous. Besides, I want to buy you an engagement ring—just a temporary one, as I shall have one made, with the stones which you shall choose for yourself.'

'You have everything worked out,' she commented, and now an edge of tartness was heard in his voice.

'Of course I have. I want to marry you, Tina. I have only once before asked a woman to marry me. When she married someone else I swore I'd never ask another woman to be my wife. I've had many women—numerous women, in fact—but none has appealed to me in the way you appeal. You have all I want in a wife.'

'Supposing that, one day, you happened to

fall in love?' Her thoughts had turned once again to the girl who was now widowed, but it was not her to whom she referred as she added, 'There might be a woman, somewhere, who will one day win your heart.'

He laughed quietly.

'A romantic way of putting it, my dear. No, I am convinced that no woman will ever win my heart. I shall be more than satisfied with my beautiful wife.'

Sincerity was in every syllable. Tina could not doubt his words, but she was realistic enough to accept the possibility of his falling in love one day. Whatever he thought now, when his desire for her was so strong that he had been driven to offer her marriage, he had no knowledge of what the future might bring. Desire without love was not a very secure foundation on which to build a marriage. And yet Tina was by no means rejecting his offer. On the contrary, she was almost resigned to the surrender which he was so confidently expecting of her.

They reached Dorchester with an hour to spare before the shops closed. She made no demur when he took her to an exclusive boutique where they sold nothing but French clothes. He bought her an evening dress of soft, azure blue velvet, with a tight-fitting bodice and

56

a gored skirt that fitted to the hips and then flared cleverly into glorious folds that swayed with the movement of her body. He bought skirts and sweaters, blouses and slacks. She was staggered at what could be done in the time available. The jewellers was still open, but Tina firmly refused to go in and look at rings.

'I must think,' she said.

'Don't you consider it's a little late for that?' The teasing was merely in the words; both his voice and his expression were serious. 'Marry me, Tina. I swear you will never regret it—' He turned as the assistant came from the shop and began fixing the security grille to the window. 'Too late—' He shrugged his shoulders. 'It's not a thing to buy in a hurry. We'll come back tomorrow morning.'

Tina said nothing. Her mind was still in a daze, for it seemed impossible that so much could have happened in a matter of a few hours. She spoke her thoughts aloud, humour entering into her for the first time.

'I feel like Cinderella,' she said as they got back into the car.

Paul laughed but said nothing. He had a satisfied look on his face which caused her to ask,

'What made you so optimistic about my marrying you?'

'I usually get what I set out to get,' he replied suavely.

'You could have asked me again to be your pillow-friend. After all, my back was to the wall, and I was becoming desperate when you found me.'

'I knew you'd refuse. Besides, I had come to want you for my wife. A man in my position should entertain and it's been remiss of me not to do it more often. I suppose, too, that I came to think that it would be pleasant to have a son who would inherit what I have to leave. Up till now I've been happy with the idea that nephews will inherit.'

Tina coloured a little at the mention of a son. Yet she felt that children would go a long way in strengthening the bond that must inevitably be between them, despite the fact that Paul would never love her.

He was speaking again, asking for her answer even though it was obvious that, having decided he would marry her, he had no intention of being rejected.

Nor did she want to reject him. Suddenly she had no fears for the future, no doubts or misgivings. And she answered softly, her face turned to his profile as he stared ahead, watching the traffic,

'I'll marry you, Paul. And—and I hope I

can—can give you everything you want of me.'
Her voice had become tremulous even though
she had hoped to keep it steady. Paul turned
to slant her a swift glance and she saw that his
lips were curved in a smile.

'I am very sure you will give me all I want,'
he said, 'all I want, and perhaps a little more.'

Did he know she was close to loving him...?
Well, it did not matter. She was sure she would
never have been able to keep it from him
anyway.

CHAPTER THREE

The aeroplane circled over the outlying districts of Heraklion and Tina, looking down, felt that all sense of thought had left her. She was married, and had had a happy honeymoon at the quaint little inn which Paul had found. It had everything—atmosphere, service, excellent food. She and Paul had slept in a four-poster bed in a quaint room that had come right out of the Middle Ages and seemed a trifle bewildered at finding itself being commercialised. It had been a time to remember, with Paul the perfect lover, gentle, yet as passionate as only a Greek could be, tender, and yet the strength of his virility was by no means painless.

She had known she was on the borderline of love; she had now stepped beyond that line, into the realms of sweet and tender adoration, and she could not help having qualms about the possible hurts that could be hers if ever her husband did happen to fall in love with someone else.

He spoke, his lips close to her ear. They were in a first-class compartment which they had all to themselves.

'Happy, my wife?'

She turned automatically and smiled at him, but shook her head at the same time.

'I can't think properly, Paul. Has it all happened, or have I been dreaming?'

'It's no dream, my dear, but reality. We're going to our home on Crete. You'll reign like a queen.'

'Tell me again about the people I'm to meet,' she begged. 'I shall feel strange, Paul, having servants about me.'

'Only for a short time,' he assured her. 'Stavros is the butler—we call him a manservant in Greece. His wife, Thoula, is one of the two maids, the other being a young woman who was widowed last year. Her name is Julia and she will be your personal maid, as I shall employ another woman in the house now. We have three gardeners and one of them, Marko, can drive the car.' His eyes strayed to the scene below. 'I hope, Tina, that you will come to love Crete as I do.'

She nodded. The plane was coming down and the land was coming up to meet it.

'But you like Athens, too.'

'I love it,' he admitted. 'My business is there,

61

so it's just as well, since I have to spend a good deal of time there.'

'You'll be away from home a lot?'

'I'm afraid so, my dear. However, you can come with me if you want. You'll be able to visit your aunt and uncle.'

'Yes, I've already thought of that.'

'They're happy at your marriage.'

'Yes. It was super that they came over to England for the wedding.'

'You made a beautiful bride, In white, my dear, you look more angel than woman.'

She coloured, as she always did when her husband flattered her. His quiet laugh was half humorous, half triumphant.

'What shall I do with myself all day?' she murmured, deliberately breaking the silence because she was embarrassed, and a trifle uneasy. This new life was going to be so different from anything she had ever known. A foreign country, dark-skinned servants whose language was not her own. A husband whose way of life in no way resembled that of men in the West. Already he had shown her who was master; already she had been warned that his word was law and that she would be far happier if she kept that in mind.

'You will have plenty to do, supervising the running of our home. The gardens are extensive, and we shall take trips on the yacht. I want to show you some of the islands, Tina. They're romantic and intriguing.'

The plane was touching down; a few small bumps and the runway was passing smoothly beneath the wheels. A car waited, with Marko at the wheel, so he was the first of the Villa Raffina's servants to whom Tina was introduced. To her surprise he was a clear-skinned blond, tall with a slender body that was clad in a pair of black trousers and a snow-white shirt rolled up above the elbows. Paul smiled at her surprise and once they were in the car he explained that Marko was a Dorian, hence his colouring.

'Most people believe that all Greeks are dark,' he went on, 'but this is not so. The Dorians in Crete live mainly on the south coast; they have changed little in three thousand years, and even today they indulge in blood feuds, so their womenfolk are scarcely ever out of mourning clothes.'

'Good heavens! These days—they kill one another?'

'The *vendetta*,' he said. 'Crete and the Mani are two places where it has survived.' He stopped and gave a light laugh. 'There's no Cretan blood in my veins,' he said presently, 'so you have no need to be afraid I shall ever do you an injury.'

She looked sideways at him and decided she would not be so sure of that. Paul, she had discovered, could be disturbingly jealous, and one evening when, walking into the dining-room at the White Hart, she had been stared at with admiration by a young man on his own at the table next to theirs, he had not been at all pleased when Tina had given the young man a smile. She had felt that Paul would have liked to shake her.

'Have we a long way to go?' asked Tina when they had been travelling for about twenty minutes.

'We cross the centre of the island,' he explained. 'Aghia Triadha is in the south of the island, on the River Yeropotamos. The Villa Raffina, as I have told you, is near the sea, yet overlooks the Plain of Tymbaki.'

'It's the Libyan Sea, you said?'

'That's right. We're usually cool in summer—cooler than most places on the island.' The car was running through a region of terraced vineyards and groves of lemons and olives. The sun was high in an azure sky and everywhere there were flowers. The car had to stop for a donkey, laden with kale and led by a little girl whose face broke into a smile as she called,

'Yasou!' then touched the donkey's flanks with the stick she carried. Paul smiled and returned the greeting. He explained to his wife that it meant 'good day' as different from good morning or goodnight.

'*Yasou* is said only in the afternoon,' he added finally.

'What is good morning?' she asked interestedly.

Kalimera. Good evening is *kalispera* and if you say *kalinikta* it means goodnight.'

She smiled then and said,

'I knew that. You've said it to me several times, Paul.'

'So I have.'

They lapsed into silence after that, with Tina, entranced by the scenery, content just to stare through the window, and take in the beauty that spread out before her. An excitement took the place of the dull apathy that seemed to have settled on her from the moment she had boarded the plane to London. It seemed so final a step she was taking and it frightened her so that she sought escape in closing her mind to it, to the future, even, and the new life on which she was embarking. She had not known Paul any time at all, and so it was natural that she should suddenly have qualms about the impulsive step she had taken. But now she was finding her

65

mind was active again, receptive to what was going on around her. The villages where women sat on steps, staring like statues into space; the children, 'showing off' by posing for the occupants of the car; the chickens foraging in the street; the huge black bull tethered to a tree in the square. Tall white companiles glistened in the sun, the silver-grey leaves of olive trees turning in the breeze so that they shone in the sunlight like so many bright, reflective surfaces.

At last the driver turned into a long avenue of palms, and the car semed to travel for more than a quarter of a mile before the snowy-white villa came into view. Tina had expected something special, but she gasped at the sheer luxury of the house that spread before her eyes. Low and long, with two wings set at right angles it stood with patrician elegance amid a galaxy of exotic tropical flowers. Terraces and parterres blazed with colour; borders flaunted scarlet hibiscus, jacaranda, poinsettias, oleanders and others too numerous to mention. The smooth green lawns were like velvet, the imposing white marble entrance gleamed in the sunshine. The front door was opened even before the car came to a standstill on the smooth surface of the forecourt where at one end a fountain played, its water stealing all the

66

colours of the rainbow and showering them in dancing disarray on to the ornamental lily-pond below.

'Oh...Paul...I'm scared...'

He laughed at her halting words, tucked a reassuring hand beneath her arm and ushered her towards the steps leading to the door, steps flanked by huge marble urns spilling over with flowers, while the columns rising behind them were wound about with brilliant magenta bougainvillaea vines. Tina was tensed up, ready to turn and run, almost. Yet the feel of her husband's hand was comforting, a reassurance against her own timidity. She lifted her eyes and saw that he was smiling. A response was not so difficult; it came spontaneously, and remained when Paul introduced her to Savros, a dark stocky Greek whose many gold fillings flashed as he spoke, welcoming her to Greece while his eyes raked her entire body in a way that caused her to colour vividly. Greek men are obsessed by sex, her aunt had declared, and Tina had suspected that she was right.

'Where are the women, Stavros?' Paul's voice had a stern inflection and Tina realised that the two women should have been here to meet their new mistress.

'They have gone to change,' explained Stavros. He spoke very good English, as did all Paul's servants. Paul was frowning as he said,

'They should have changed earlier. Call them!' Imperious the tone, and the flick of his hand was arrogantly authoritative. 'At once!'

'Yes, Mr Paul.'

Paul had already explained that the servants used first names, so Tina must expect to be addressed as Mrs Paul, or Kyria Paul, and not as Mrs Christos.

The women came down, both flustered and apologetic.

Paul eyed them sternly but made no comment. Tina guessed that they would be admonished later, when she was not present. She was introduced to them, welcomed to Crete, and then she was being shown up to the room which she would share with her husband. It was large and airy, with a window taking up the whole of one wall, a sliding window that opened on to a balcony dripping with flowers. The view was to olive slopes and of course the gorgeous wine-dark sea of Greece. Tina caught her breath as her eyes moved back from the sea to the gardens, and then to one side where the olive slopes basked in the sunshine.

So peaceful! Thoula had left the room and Tina was alone for a few moments. She brought her gaze into the room, taking in the expensive drapes and carpet, both of which were white. The furniture was of bird's-eye maple, the matching bed of outside proportions and covered with a beautifully embroidered counterpane which Tina suspected had once formed part of the expensive dowry of some relative of Paul's. He had told her that he had a mother living but no father. His mother lived with her aged sister on the island of Patmos and Paul promised to take Tina there in the not-too-distant future. He entered and she turned, a smile fluttering to her lips. He strode into the room, kicking the door closed behind him. He opened his hands, an order for her to go to him, which she did, and found herself crushed to his hard body, her lips taken with all the arrogant possession that was already familiar to her. She responded, her body on fire within minutes. Paul crushed one breast within his hand; she quivered to the warmth, to the exquisite pain inflicted by his strength. He was so tall above her, so dominant. She swayed within the circle of his arms, pressing her slender body to his in a gesture of complete surrender. He laughed softly and said he was glad he had married her.

'To have had you for a pillow-friend would not have been the same,' he admitted, his voice a little hoarse from the passion that was only partly being kept in check. 'Just think—you in one house and me in another! It was a mad idea when I want you so much!' His mouth, hard and demanding, came down on hers, forcing her lips apart. 'I must thank you for holding out, my lovely, desirable Tina!' He had drawn away slightly; she saw the fire of passion in his eyes and her own desire swelled to flood every fibre of her body. To want a man so much must surely be destructive in the end, she thought, tempting him with her eyes, her body, her lips. He resisted, to her amazement, and said, softly, purringly, his mouth caressing her ear,

'Love is for night time...The moon is full tonight; it floods this side of the house. I shall make love to you by moonlight...'

He moved and she followed him with her eyes as he went to a door which she had noticed but not opened. It led to another bedroom, and she went slowly towards it as Paul passed through the door. It was essentially a man's room, with a single bed, a desk by the window, an easy chair richly upholstered in dark green damask. The carpet was thick and dark; the drapes of leaf-green linen were drawn right back so that the sun's rays, slanting now as the afternoon drew to its close, filled the room. A bathroom lay to one side, so this suite consisted of two bedrooms and two bathrooms, Tina realised. She said, automatically indicating the bed,

'Did you sleep here?'

He nodded his head.

'Yes. This house was designed to accommodate two married couples who were bosom friends. They each had a suite like this.'

'So you didn't have the house built?' she said in surprise.

'No, I couldn't get a site quite like this one. There are some alterations that I had planned and never carried out. I expect I shall do so now that I'm married—' He paused and smiled a little mockingly. 'We shall be needing a nursery suite, I guess, before very long.'

'I hope I shall not disappoint you.' Her tone was expressionless, she was not particularly enamoured by the prospect of having a child just yet.

'I don't think you will, my dear.'

'You're very confident.'

'Unless there's something radically wrong with one of us I expect we shall be parents within the year.' So coldly clinical! Tina felt a pang of disappointment and yet there was anger there as well. Was that the way he was thinking about her already?—as a woman whose prime function was to produce children?

Something made her say tartly.

'I believe all Greek men want sons. What happens if I produce only daughters?'

He shrugged but frowned as well.

'I should be disappointed, but there would be nothing I could do about it.'

'It's the man who determines the sex,' she told him.

'Been reading up your biology, eh?'

'I'm just making sure I'm not blamed if only girls come along.'

Her husband's frown deepened.

'What's the matter with you?' he demanded. 'You've become fractious all at once.' She said nothing and after a space he added with mock sternness, 'Fractious little girls get spanked—and at this moment you certainly look like a little girl, with that pout and that truculent expression.' He came to her, and stood over her. 'Smile,' he ordered. 'let me see the end of these tantrums!'

She managed a shaky laugh, but laughter was by no means as spontaneous as her smile had been a few minutes previously. She was angry without quite knowing why; there was a resentment growing within her for which there was no accounting. Paul had a right to expect children; she had known this from the start. Why, then, should she be reacting in this way?

He took her hand and drew her to him. She was given a playful slap before being kissed.

'You're tired,' he decided, holding her from him. 'Is that why you're feeling bad-tempered?'

'I'm not bad-tempered.' She wanted to cry, so she supposed she must be tired, since there was absolutely nothing to cry for...or was there? Could it be that she was regretting that she had married a man who did not love her? A sigh quivered on her lips. She had known he had no love for her. He had admitted it, so why she should be feeling like this was beyond her comprehension. She had a beautiful home, servants, a handsome husband...'I'm sorry,' she said contritely. 'I must be tired, as you say.'

'Then have a rest,' he advised. 'You'll feel more like enjoying the evening if you are refreshed by sleep.'

He left her and she looked around his room, wondering if he would ever use it again. She supposed not; perhaps he would keep it as a dressing-room, or perhaps a study, she thought, her eyes catching the desk again. At last she turned, to stand in the doorway of the larger room, surveying the beautiful furniture, the expensive décor, the view from the window. She went to the bathroom and again gave a little gasp. Thick carpet surrounding a circular bath sunken into the floor; gold-plated fittings and mirrors on the walls. A large potted palm tree stood in a corner, its fronds bending over one part of the bath. There were flowers growing in small marble urns, delightful tiled insets of mermaids on the walls. The curtains were full and frilly, there was a chair upholstered in cerise velvet to match the carpet. Expensive towels as big as sheets, bottles of bath oil, jars of talc, tablets of soap...all new and unopened. She realised that Paul must have arranged for all this to be done before he went to England. He had been so sure that he would bring back a bride with him...

Dinner was served in a high-ceilinged room with modern dining-table and chairs of the most luxurious make and design. The carpet was thick to the feet; the walls were lined with rose-peach silk. Stavros and Thoula waited on the table with Julia bringing in the different courses. Paul, amused at Tina's rather awe-struck manner, told her softly to relax, as this was what she must become used to from now on. He himself was so serenely cool, so perfectly at ease amid all this incredible luxury. Tina waited until they were alone before saying,

'It'll take a good deal of getting used to, Paul. I feel in a daze, and I'm very sure I shall be feeling this way for a long time to come.'

'A week, perhaps,' he said casually. 'The hotel you were in in Athens was very plush, you know.'

'Hotels are different from homes.'

'A little,' he conceded.

'I keep thinking it isn't true.' Her lips parted in a lovely winning smile as she looked at him across the candlelit table. 'I'm afraid I shall wake up to find myself in Mrs France-Cobet's kitchen.'

'I'd rather you didn't mention that woman again,' said her husband crisply. 'You ought never to have taken such a degrading kind of job!'

'There was nothing else.'

'We'll forget it, Tina!'

She averted her eyes, colouring at his sternness. It was a relief when Stavros entered with the sweet course. He had soon gone, though, and once again Tina was alone with her husband. He was silent, gazing at the straw-coloured wine in his glass. Tina felt a restlessness creep over her; she wished she could know what he was thinking about. He was impassive, absorbed in the glass he held. The silence stretched and it was as if he suddenly became aware of it because he glanced up, to meet her gaze. He drained his glass, then picked up his dessert spoon.

'Can we go for a walk afterwards?' she asked, and he nodded at once.

'I usually take a stroll in the grounds after dinner,' he told her. 'The air's cool and fresh after the heat of the afternoon. It's pleasant to feel the sea breeze, too.' .

As he had said, the moon was full, and as they strolled in the sweet-scented gardens of the villa, its argent light seemed to illuminate everything around them. It was a magical setting, a backcloth for romance. Tina felt her husband's fingers curl around hers, was aware of the ardour that would soon be released. His voice was tender as he said,

'The first night in our own home, my wife. Are you as happy as I am?'

She swung round to face him and they both stopped.

'Are you happy, Paul—really happy?'

'What a question!' His soft laugh was like music in her ears, for there seemed to be a wealth of tenderness contained in it. 'Of course I am happy. Haven't I got everything a man could want?'

Everything...Tina felt a sadness mingle with the pleasure which his tender laugh had given her. Paul did have all he wanted...but then he did not want love...

She sighed, but pressed close to him just the

same. She needed the comfort of his body and as his arms came about her she was potently aware of his nearness, of the sound of his heart beating in the deep silence. She glanced around, at the hills with their olive trees forming strange silhouettes against the silver-tinted sky. The silence seemed to widen and then was broken by the bray of a lonely donkey on a hillside. It seemed to be the signal for the cicadas to begin their whirring noise in the trees and for Paul to whisper, his lips caressing her cheek,

'Let's go back, dear. It's getting late anyway.' He turned and they retraced their steps. The air was beautifully cool and perfumed; the fountain, illuminated with coloured lights, made music as it fell into the pool. Tina could have remained outside in this magical setting for a while longer, but she sensed her husband's impatience, his deep desire to have her in his arms.

The servants were not about when they entered the villa, and they went straight to their room. Tina melted into Paul's arms immediately he had closed the door, and lifted her face for his kiss. Her heart seemed to swell with love for him, her body longed to be possessed. He whispered to her, his voice becoming vibrant with desire. She felt his lips close to her throat, knew the sheer ecstasy of hand seeking the firm contour of her breast. His body pressed close, hard and demanding, dominant with all the arrogance of a conqueror. His hand left her breast to fumble with the fasteners of her dress; it slipped to the floor and she stepped out of it. His eyes wandered, devouring every seductive curve that was revealed through the sheer transparency of her underwear. His hands were removing again; she coloured painfully as another garment was removed. And a little while later, his passion flared to ignite hers, he lifted her and carried her to the bed. The curtains were wide apart and the moonbeams flooded into the room, illuminating it with magic and mystery...and in that setting they made love, just as Paul had promised, Tina, thrilling to every caress, found for the first time that she herself could caress, and the pleasure, she gave proved the prelude to her own complete fulfilment.

CHAPTER FOUR

They had been married just six weeks when Paul said he would take Tina to Patmos to see his mother.

'She wasn't too happy at the idea of my marrying an English girl,' he admitted, but went on to say grimly that his choice of wife was his own affair and not his mother's. 'She was let down in some way by an Englishwoman she befriended once, when she was young,' continued Paul by way of explanation. 'I never did discover what it was all about. Mother was obviously upset, though, because the experience gave her a permanent dislike of the English.'

Tina looked dismayed.

'It looks very much as if she won't like me, Paul.'

'We'll see,' he returned briefly, and changed the subject, saying that before they went to Patmos he had business to attend to in Athens. He had been there on several occasions, and Tina had accompanied him on all but one of those occasions. She had been off colour and preferred to stay at home. Paul, anxious about her, said he would not go but the business that was taking him there was very urgent. This time, she would be going with him. She wanted to see her aunt and uncle, for one thing, and for another she had some shopping to do.

They flew early in the morning and she was with her aunt and uncle for lunch, while Paul went off to his business conference. Aunt Doris asked how she was getting along—she always did ask this, reflected Tina with some amusement—and was assured that her niece was happy. Tina had not told her aunt that Paul did not love her. It was something to be kept to herself for ever.

'Well, I must say that Paul's a changed man,' declared Aunt Doris. 'He did have a reputation, I know. Women just ran after him, that was the trouble.'

'I expect they still do,' interposed Uncle Frank. 'It's not feasible that his marriage has made much difference to those who set their caps at him. Besides, there'll be many who still believe he's single.'

The thought had occurred to Tina, but she trusted Paul implicitly. He would never have a pillow-friend while he had a wife.

'We want you to come for a visit,' she said. 'I expect you'll want to leave it until later, though, seeing that you're still getting tourists coming in.'

'The tourists seem to come all the year round these days,' said her aunt. 'Supposing we come about a fortnight before Christmas?'

'Yes, that'll be fine. You'll have a surprise when you see the villa. It's the very last thing in luxury!'

'You're a very fortunate young lady,' smiled her uncle. 'We never thought, when we invited you over, that you'd capture a Greek millionaire! Mind you, you're pretty enough to capture any man—'

'Uncle,' she broke in, laughing, 'spare my blushes!'

'Paul obviously thinks you're beautiful,' commented Aunt Doris musingly. 'He's choosy, that one. It's always been said that as he's a perfectionist himself he demands perfection in his servants, his employees here in the city, and in the women he takes—or, I should say, has taken—as his lights o' love.'

Tina coloured a little, yet the fact that her husband had a reputation had never worried her in the least. So long as he remained faithful to her, his past was his own affair.

After lunch she went out to the shops, then on up to the Acropolis. She was to meet Paul around six o'clock and as he had given her a key to his flat she went on there after leaving the Acropolis. Paul had a man-servant who looked after the flat, but today was his day off. It did not matter, Paul had said, because they would be dining out anyway. She had just got in when to her surprise the bell rang. She went to the door, to be confronted by a tall dark Greek girl who after giving a slight start of surprise looked Tina over from head to foot and said curtly,

'Who are you?' and before Tina could reply, 'Is Paul in?' The dark eyes flickered past Tina to the hall beyond.

'No, he isn't.' Tina looked at her, noticing the rare and subtle beauty of the classical features, the big dark eyes that seemed to hold a mystery in their depths, the clear skin, pale bronze and tightly-drawn over high cheekbones. Tina judged the girl's age to be about twenty-eight or nine; she wondered who she was and why she was here.

'Who are you?' enquired the girl again, her manner almost insolent as she looked Tina over for the second time.

'I'm his wife,' answered Tina softly. 'And who are you?'

'His wife!' The girl's voice was suddenly a rasp, harsh and gratingly sharp. 'His *wife*!'

Tina felt her temper rising. Was this one of

those pillow-friends that had come and gone?

'Yes, his wife. And now, if you'll excuse me—' Tina got no further. To her amazement the girl brushed past her and entered the hall, swinging round and glowering at Tina.

'So he did get married? He threatened he would. Well, I don't know how he came to marry an English girl, but I might as well tell you that he married you simply to spite me!'

Icicles seemed to be clinging to Tina's spine. She heard herself say, in a choked little voice,

'Who are you?'

'I'm...' Her voice trailed and Tina swung round to come face to face with her husband. He might not have noticed her, for his eyes were on the lovely face of the girl who stood behind Tina, a girl who was head and shoulders taller than she.

'Dora—what are you doing here?'

'I came to see you—' She spread a hand towards Tina and her voice broke a little as she added, 'I have just met your—your wife.'

'I see...' He gazed at Tina. She was watching him closely, the name Dora ringing in her ears. But Dora Vassilou lived in Crete...He seemed to have a sudden dryness in his mouth, for she saw his lips working, as if he were trying to moisten them, 'Tina,' he said at length, 'this is Dora Vassilou, an old friend of mine.'

Neither girl spoke. It was a tense, glacier-cold silence, broken at last by Paul, who flicked a hand and invited them into the sitting-room.

'I happened to be in Athens,' Dora managed presently, 'and thought you might be at the flat, so I called.' She was standing by the high window, staring at Paul across the room. 'You didn't say anything about getting married when last I saw you...and stayed here, in the flat.' She paused a moment, her eyes flickering to Tina, who was standing close to her husband, her face as white as her blouse, her small hands clenched tightly at her sides. 'It was about six weeks ago—no, perhaps a little more, wasn't it? How long have you been married, Paul?'

'Just over six weeks.' His face was tight; Tina could not have said whether he was angry or merely uncomfortable. For her—she was thinking of the time element just mentioned by Dora. She stayed here, with Paul, just over six weeks ago...

'I think,' said Tina in a hollow little voice, 'I'd better leave you alone. I'm sure you have things to talk about.' And without giving Paul the chance to speak she brushed past him and was in the street within seconds.

She walked and walked, in the loneliness of misery, her tangled thoughts one moment telling her that what Paul had done prior to their marriage was none of her business, but the next moment she was hearing him saying that he wanted her—Tina—more than any other woman he had ever known. He had come to her in England and offered her marriage. She had naturally taken it for granted that he had not had any other woman between the time when she had left Greece and the time when he had seen her in England. Yet he had slept with his old flame only a few nights before he decided to ask Tina to marry him.

Disgusted, she continued to walk, increasing the distance between herself and the flat. Her eyes were filled with tears; she did stop to wonder what she intended to do and although it occurred to her that she could go to her uncle's hotel, she dismissed the idea at once. She had no wish to upset either her aunt or her uncle. Besides, she had a strong suspicion that they would tell her to mind her own business, that what Paul did before his marriage was his concern, not hers.

She had no idea how long she had walked, but she suddenly realised she was on totally unfamiliar ground. It was quieter, more residential. She stopped, only to begin hurrying on again as she saw a dark, stockily built Greek coming purposefully towards her from the other side of the tree-lined road. He followed her and she began to run, her heart throbbing painfully, the tears streaming down her face. She had never felt so depressed in her life, no, not even when she was working for Mrs France-Cobet. The man's footsteps were no longer to be heard and she slowed down, glancing behind her. She wanted to turn back, to try to find her way...to where? Her nerves were drawn to threads of fear and uncertainty. All was bleak, hopeless, dark. She was so sunk in the depths of despair that she convinced herself that there was no going back to her husband. In the end she decided she must go to her uncle's hotel. It was stupid to wander about like this, feeling sorry for herself, telling herself she had nowhere to go. The man appeared to have gone and she turned back, hurrying along the road towards the more brightly illuminated part of the outskirts of the town. And luckily she saw a roving taxi and hailing it, was relieved to see it slowing down. She got in, giving the name of her uncle's hotel. Within a quarter of an hour she was there, noticing the surprised look on the face of the receptionist as he saw her alone. It was gone nine o'clock, she realised. She had been walking for three hours.

She hurried along to her aunt's private sitting room, but reaching the door she stopped. What was she going to say? How would her aunt and uncle take it when she said she had left her husband? Well, it had to be done, she decided, resolutely lifting a hand to knock on the door. She opened it and went in, saw the look of surprised enquiry on her aunt's face and burst into tears.

'What...?' Aunt Doris had been reading by the electric fire, but she rose at once and came towards her niece, her round, homely face anxious, her arms outstretched.

'I've left Paul...' The lump in her throat choked any further words which Tina might have uttered. She was clasped to her aunt's bosom and for a few moments she wept unrestrainedly, almost oblivious of the soothing words being spoken, or the gentle pats which her aunt was giving her on the back and on the shoulder.

'Tell me all about it, dear,' Aunt Doris said gently when at last Tina's sobs had abated and her tears were dried. 'You've quarrelled?'

Tina shook her head.

'No, we—we haven't.' She felt foolish all at once, and it was a long while before she could bring herself to explain.

'You walked out, just for that?' Aunt Doris seemed as if she could not believe the evidence of her own ears. 'You've left your husband for a reason like that?'

Tina said nothing for a while and then, 'Can I stay here, Auntie?'

'Of course—but, Tina, you can't leave Paul...' Her voice trailed away and her eyes went past Tina to the door.

Tina spun around, her face blanching.

'Paul—' Her voice caught on the word and she started to cry again.

'I'll leave you to sort it out,' decided Aunt Doris, preparing to depart. 'Have you seen Frank, Paul?'

'Yes. He's busy in the restaurant. I asked him if Tina was here and he said no—not that he knew of. He told me to come and see you.' He sounded impatient, and his eyes were hard as they rested on his wife's tear-stained face.

Aunt Doris passed quietly from the room, closing the door behind her. Paul stood some distance from his wife, staring at her through those hard eyes of his. She shivered seeing in him all that was pagan.

Paul was the first to break the silence, his voice hard and inflexible as he said.

'What do you mean by running away like that? I've been searching everywhere for you. I did think of coming here but felt you'd not bring your relatives into it, so I was reluctant to contact them. I did it as a last resort.' He paused as if suddenly angry with himself for

troubling to explain. 'Why did you run off?'
he asked again.

She raised her head, conscious of her hot
cheeks, her tear-dimmed eyes.

'I was—disgusted.'

Silence for a long moment and then,

'Is that all you have to say?'

It seemed so inadequate now, she realised.
Not only inadequate, but nonsensical.

'It was awful, her coming there, and mentioning having slept with you—only a very short
time before you came to me, asking me to
marry you. I took it for granted that you'd
been—been faithful—' She broke off, shrugg-
ing in an attempt to hide her embarrassment.
For she was embarrassed, very. She felt foolish,
knowing that she had attached far too much
importance to the whole affair.

His eyes were points of flint as he said,

'I wasn't aware that Dora had mentioned
anything about sleeping with me.'

Tina gave a slight start.

'I assumed that, having stayed the night at
the flat, she had slept with you.'

Paul's face became as dark and cold as
ironstone.

'Then you assume too much,' he said frigidly. 'Dora did not sleep with me on that
occasion—on others, yes, I make no denial of

89

that. But I'll remind you of this, Tina, even if I had slept with Dora, it had absolutely nothing to do with you.' He paused, looking directly at her. 'What I did before my marriage is my own affair, and I'll thank you to keep out of it.' So tall and overpowering he seemed, and stern to the point of harshness. His voice had been quiet but carrying a magisterial quality which was a dark warning in itself. She said, in a muffled little voice,

'I'm sorry. I took it for granted that you and she had slept together.'

'I've just told you,' he said sharply, 'that you take too much for granted! I told you also that whatever I did before my marriage has nothing to do with you. And now if you're ready we'll go home. Go and find your aunt.'

She hesitated, looking up at him. His face was a blur through the tears in her eyes, but the sternness seemed still to be there, and not a sign of pity, or of concern for her feelings. But through the tangle of her thoughts she was admitting that she did not deserve pity. She moved to the door, saying with a little access of desolation,

'I'll tell Auntie that we—er—we've made it up.'

'You told her we'd quarrelled?'

She shook her head.

'No, I told her the truth—that I'd walked out because of—of Dora.' She hung her head beneath the dark censure of his gaze. 'I'll be back in a minute,' she added, and hastily left the room.

If Paul meant to punish her he succeeded. There were three bedrooms in the flat and he and Tina had hitherto shared the largest on their visits to Athens. Tina went to it, and after showering and putting on a nightgown she waited, by the window, for him to join her. She heard him moving, going into the other bathroom, then the adjoining bedroom. The finality of a closing door was the stab that pierced her heart and caused her to weep again, weep with the abandonment of loss. This was the first time her husband had been really angry with her and it hurt excruciatingly. He had not troubled to tell her what had happened after she left the flat. She would probably never know what transpired between him and his old flame. She told herself that she did not want to know, and yet at the same time she was aware of a sense of curiosity, remembering as she did the girl's very definite assertion that Paul had married her, Tina, simply to spite Dora.

She got into bed at last, but spent a restless

night, with intervals of wakefulness and fitful dozing. She had looked forward to this trip, just as she had looked forward to the others that had gone before, but through her own folly she had spoiled it all.

The sun was shining into the room as she awoke from her last troubled sleep; she got up, listening for a sign of movement from the next room, but all was quiet. She bathed and dressed, then went to the breakfast-room. Paul was there, about to make some toast. She asked where his manservant was.

'Sometimes, when it's his day off, he stays the night with his married sister. He did not know we'd be here.' Voice was abrupt, unfriendly. Tina asked if she could do anything and was told she could make the coffee. She went into the kitchen, her heart heavy within her. There must be some way of getting back to that blissful relationship, but she could not find it. Paul was cool and quiet over breakfast; he bade her a brief good morning afterwards and went out, saying he would not be back until seven o'clock that evening.

Her mouth trembled as she watched him go. He had not kissed her, but she had not expected him to. His features had retained that hard impassivity that was on his face last night, an expression she was seeing for the very first time. She was learning about him—and she supposed he was learning about her...things he did not like.

There was nothing to do but go out. She found her steps directed to her uncle's hotel. Her aunt, eager for news of what had transpired, left her job of supervising the flower arrangements and took her niece to her private room.

'Sit down, child—' She scanned Tina's pale face and frowned. 'What's happened? Where's Paul?'

'He has business to attend to. I didn't expect him to be with me in the daytime.' Tina sat down, wishing her heart was not so heavy, her mind so full of frightening thoughts. Yes, she was frightened—that her husband might already be regretting his marriage to her.

'What happened?' enquired her aunt again, ringing the bell to bring one of the staff so that she could order coffee.

Tina coloured as she said.

'Paul was still angry when we arrived at the flat. He—decided to sleep in—in the other room.' Her words caught on a little sob which brought a sigh to her aunt's lips. 'I asked for it,' she added desolately. 'I assumed he had slept with Dora, but he hadn't.'

'Why was she there, then?'

'He didn't say, but it seems feasible that she was in Athens and called to see him, and stayed the night—in one of the other bedrooms, that is.'

'Yes, that is feasible, as you say.' There was a definite edge of scepticism in Aunt Doris's voice which did not escape her niece. Tina tried not to allow doubts to enter her mind, but realised that they were doing so. Until her aunt spoke she had taken her husband's word as the truth, but now...Men were all liars, her aunt had once said. Could Paul be lying? If he was then what right had he to adopt that attitude of the injured party, treating his wife with cold disdain?

'I think I'll go and do some shopping, Auntie,' she said, feeling she must get out of here, away by herself, to think.

If she stayed here she would be expected to talk, and the tumult of her thoughts at the present time was not for putting into words.

'Do you have some shopping to do, Tina, or are you just saying that?'

'I want to be on my own, Auntie.'

But the older woman was shaking her head.

'It wouldn't be good for you at this time, love. Stay here; let Paul come here for you— You can phone him when you know he'll be at the flat. I shall speak to him—'

94

'No,' broke in Tina. 'I wouldn't like that—nor would Paul. He was angry enough when he learned that I'd told you everything.'

Her aunt gave a small sigh.

'He's a strange man, Tina, coming from a strange part of Greece. There's no knowing what his characteristics are, not with his ancestry being what it is.'

'He doesn't go there,' returned Tina, suddenly urged to defend him. 'He's very cultured, as you know—Westernised, to a great extent.'

'I concede a point there, but it's a case of heredity. He is what he is, and although environment plays a great part in the forming of a man's character it's been proved that heredity's stronger. You could keep a tiger in captivity for ever, but you'd never tame it.'

Tina had to smile.

'That's an extreme case, Auntie,' she said.

'The Greeks were pagans, my dear.'

'Weren't we all, at one time?'

'Well, that's another point I'm willing to concede—' She stopped on hearing a knock on the door. 'Come in,' she called, and gave the order to the dark Greek who entered.

'Just coffee, Mrs Frank?'

'And a few biscuits, Georgios, please.'

He was back within five minutes and the

coffee was served to them.

'Are you going to stay here?' her aunt was saying a moment or two later, when the man had departed.

'I feel so restless, Auntie. I'd get on your nerves.'

'It would have been better,' remarked Aunt Doris wisely, 'if you hadn't come with him this time.'

Tina thought so too, yet on the other hand she would rather know that Dora was in the habit of calling on Paul when she was in Athens. Not that she would always find him in residence at the flat, of course, but on those occasions when he was she would obviously be welcome, or otherwise she would not be calling. Of course, mused Tina, the girl had not known that Paul was married, and it could very well be that she would never call again. Certainly she would be shy of calling if she knew that Paul's wife would be there.

'He wants me to meet his mother,' said Tina, changing the subject. 'We'll be going on the yacht.'

Her aunt looked surprised.

'I didn't know he had a mother. Where does she live?'

'On the island of Patmos.'

'The smallest of the Dodecanese islands—a

beautiful island, Tina, you'll adore it!'

'You've been there, then?'

She nodded her head.

Your uncle and I went there last year—
Didn't I mention it in any of my letters?'

'No, I'm sure you didn't. Is it as nice as
Crete?'

'It's vastly different. There's a famous
monastery there with some very beautiful
frescoes. The village of Chora's interesting too.
You'll see Byzantine-style houses, and you'll
be able to buy the most exquisite hand
embroidery.'

'Paul's mother lives in Chora,' said Tina
meditatively, 'with her sister.'

'I hope she likes you, dear.'

Tina's mouth curved with a hint of doubt.

'Paul says she doesn't care much for the
English.'

Her aunt grimaced.

'To the devil with her, then. Doesn't she
speak the language?'

'I don't know; Paul didn't say.' Tina drained
her cup and placed it on the saucer. 'I'm going
out, Auntie,' she stated firmly, rising as she
spoke.

'Very well, love. Will you come back and
have lunch with us?'

'Yes, I'd like that. In the restaurant?'

Aunt Doris shook her head.

'No, in here. Your uncle and I like a little privacy. It makes a nice break in the middle of the day.' She paused, looking anxiously at her niece. 'Don't brood, child, promise me?'

Tina managed a smile as she said,

'I promise, Auntie. I'll try to find something interesting to do.'

CHAPTER FIVE

More by natural instinct than design Tina's steps took her to the Acropolis. For although there were still many tourists despite the lateness of the season, she knew she would find the peace there which her mind craved. She stood gazing up at the Parthenon, the sun on her hair and warm on her face. A crowd of tourists with a guide came and stood close and she decided to move, scarcely aware that a young man was also moving away from the crowd, with their snapping cameras and the hoarse voice of the female guide coming from within their midst.

He spoke to her, frowning a little and gesturing back, to where they had been before the tourists appeared.

'I'd love to come here one day and find myself the lone occupant of the site. Crowds drive me to distraction.' He smiled at her; she noticed the frank blue eyes set wide apart, the straight nose and firm chin. He was dressed neatly yet casually in denims and a fresh striped shirt. His camera was slung across his back. Tina looked away, feeling somehow that she ought not to be speaking to a strange young man. Yet she answered him for all that, and managed to produce a smile at the same time.

'I too would like to come here when there's no other person about, I expect you could, if you came early enough in the morning.'

'The site isn't open, though.'

'No, that the trouble.'

He looked at her, hesitating before asking if she were on holiday. He added before she could answer,

'Are you alone?'

'No, my husband's in Athens, but on business. I'm finding my own amusement until this evening.' She liked the frankness in his manner, the ready smile. And it was so nice to be talking to an Englishman. 'Are you on holiday?'

'Yes. I had to take a late one this year, so I thought I'd come to Greece. It's not too cold yet, but not so hot either. I was here once in July and it was exhausting.'

'Yes, I've experienced the July heat.'

'You live here, in Athens?'

Tina shook her head?

'No we live on the island of Crete. Have you been there?'

'Yes, briefly. I was on a cruise and they gave us just enough time to visit the palace at Knosses. It was the thrill of a lifetime—but I'd have liked to see some more of the island.' He paused for a moment. 'You must be staying in Athens?'

'Yes, we are. My husband has a flat there—' She stopped aware that it must sound strange to say that her husband had a flat instead of saying '*we* have a flat.'

'It must be nice to live here.' His glance was one of admiration now. 'Your husband—he's English?'

She made no answer for a while feeling that the young man was asking too many questions. And yet there was really no offence meant, she thought, and answered quietly.

'No, he's Greek.'

The blue eyes widened a little, but he made no comment, saying instead,

'Are you having lunch? I mean,' he added hastily, 'if you like, we could have it together?'

Tina began to shake her head, then stopped. This few minutes' chat had lifted some of the weight from her heart and she found herself reluctant to put an abrupt end to it.

'I'm going to my uncle's hotel in Constitution Square,' she said. 'You can come if you want.'

His eyes lit with eagerness.

'He wouldn't mind?'

'No, of course not.' The words were out before Tina remembered that they were to eat in her aunt's private sitting-room and not the restaurant. Oh, well, she was still sure that Aunt Doris would not mind—in fact, she would be only to happy to have an Englishman for lunch, as there weren't many English tourists just now; they were mainly Germans and Americans.

'Shall we get a taxi?' asked the young man.

'For myself, I'd rather walk.'

'Fine. So would I?' He told her his name and then asked her hers.

'Tina,' was all she offered.

'Tina...That's a pretty name. Can I use it?'

'Yes,' she answered briefly.

'And you will call me Bill, won't you?'

She nodded as they began to move towards the Propylaea, which was in ancient times the ceremonial entrance to the sacred hill. Tina was silent as they went down the steps, her thoughts on Paul, with the question uppermost in her mind being, quite naturally, what would his reaction be were he to learn that she was with this young man. She had already witnessed his jealousy...and that resulted merely from her giving a young man a smile! She shrugged inwardly. It was a hundred to one chance of Paul's ever finding out that she had spent a few hours in a man's company.

Her aunt looked a trifle uneasy when Tina, having asked Bill to wait in the lobby of the hotel, went to find her and told her that she had a friend whom she would like to bring to lunch.

'It's a man,' Tina added as the thought occurred to her. And it was then that Aunt Doris frowned and looked uneasy.

'Would Paul approve?' she wanted to know. 'How did you come to meet him anyway?'

Tina explained briefly, adding that Paul would never know, so the question of his approval or disapproval did not arise.

'Is this retaliation?' demanded her aunt bluntly.

'No—the idea never occurred to me.'

'Not consciously, perhaps. Where is the young man?'

'In the lobby. Er—If you'd rather we ate in the restaurant, Auntie, please say so.' Tina looked anxiously at her, feeling now that perhaps she had been too presumptuous in deciding that her aunt would not mind having Bill to lunch.

'As a matter of fact, Tina, your uncle and I have already decided we'd lunch in the restaurant, as we've had to send no fewer than three of the staff home this morning. There's a bug about and a lot of people are affected by it.'

'Oh, so we're all eating in the restaurant?'

Her aunt nodded. The table was in a far corner, snug and secluded behind a screen of potted palms of luxurious growth. Bill thought the hotel was very plush, far different from the 'budget' one in which he was staying in Omonia Square.

'I like Omonia Square,' said Tina. 'All the cafés and hotels seem to be swarming with bootblacks and people selling all sorts of souvenirs, and flowers. It's an exciting place.'

'Very different,' said Uncle Frank, 'but intriguing. I agree with Tina that it's exciting.'

'Shall we go there afterwards?' suggested Bill, looking at Tina and so missing the glance that passed between her aunt and uncle.

'If you like.' Tina thought it would help to pass the day, and also it would take her mind off her troubles, preventing her from dwelling on the evening when she and Paul would meet at the flat. She kept wondering how he would be with her, and if he had got over his ill-humour by now.

Omonia Square was teeming with life; there

were Greek seamen mingling with Scandinavian tourists, peddlers shouting their wares among the hive of workmen's *cafenions*. Men sprawled at the café tables, smoking while they played *tavla* or twirled their worry beads. Bill knew of a restaurant that was better than the rest and they went and had refreshments on the terrace. From there they had a superb view of the Acropolis, dominating the city, its temples golden in the sunshine. Tina enjoyed herself and when Bill asked if she would be free the following day she found herself unhesitatingly saying yes, and arranging to meet him in Constitution Square. If he was curious as to why she should be willing to go about with him he hid it successfully, grateful that he had found such a pleasant companion.

'Thank you for a most interesting day,' he said earnestly when he left her. 'It gets a bit boring sometimes, when you're on your own, I find.'

She nodded and smiled.

'I agree. While I'm one of those who can amuse myself, I also find that having company makes a difference.'

They parted, to go their separate ways, and almost at once Tina felt the heavy weight descend upon her again. She dragged her steps the nearer she got to the flat, and knew an overwhelming relief to find Paul had not yet come in. She would compose herself in the bath. When she came out he still had not arrived and she frowned as she glanced at the clock. A quarter past seven...Another ten minutes went by, and then another. At a quarter to eight he arrived, looking immaculate as usual but tired. She said timidly,

'Did you have a good day, Paul?'

He gave her a perfunctory nod.

'Yes, good but wearying.' He put his brief-case on the couch and looked at her. 'Have you enjoyed your day?'

She nodded dumbly, turning away. She would not let him see the tears that were gathering in her eyes. She suspected that he knew she loved him, madly, wildly, so he knew too that this attitude he was adopting hurt with agonising intensity. He was cruel, uncaring that he tore her heart in two. Fool that she was to fall in love with him! And bigger fool to let him see it. She had presented him with a weapon that he could employ ruthlessly just whenever he liked. Well, the only thing was to *pretend* she did not love him, and if she could put on an effective act his weapon would no longer be a weapon at all.

'I had a most interesting day.' Defiance in her voice, and a certain element of lightness as

well. 'I had lunch with Aunt and Uncle...'
Fleetingly she paused, irresolute, and then,
with swift resolve unless she changed her mind,
'I met a charming young man on the Acropolis
and invited him along as well. We made a four-
some, it was very pleasant.' She was still turned
from him but tensed in every nerve, unable to
hazard a guess as to what his reaction might
be. She heard the one word, murmured vibrat-
ingly through his teeth,
'*What?*'
She turned, feigning surprise.
'Didn't you hear me, Paul?' She scanned the
dark satanic features and quivered from head
to foot. God, is he going to murder me? she
thought, her nerves all knotted up inside her.
'I was telling you about a young man I met.
He was English—Bill is his name...' She trailed off, swallowing convulsively in an attempt
to remove the little ball of fear that was block-
ing her throat. Flashing through the disordered
tangle of her mind she knew she ought to have
practised more caution. She was going to suffer for that little show of challenging defiance.
   She wanted to run as he came closer—oh, so
menacingly—but her legs were jelly beneath
her, likely to give way any moment now. Yet
anger rose alongside her fear. She had always
experienced anger if ever she was frightened,

white-hot anger against the person, or thing, that had put fear into her. Her anger showed in her eyes; they blazed and she was not to know that she might have escaped but for her sudden change of expression, was not aware that the fire was to ignite a fury that, although smouldering dangerously, might have been extinguished by the sheer will-power of the man possessed of it.

He strode across the distance separating them, gripped her mercilessly by the shoulders and shook her without ceasing until he himself was out of breath. She cried out in protest, then wept and begged him to stop. Finally she was sobbing piteously, holding on to her balance only because of his ruthless grip upon her arms. He flung her from him, his face twisted with fury. She staggered back and would have fallen, but just in time he caught her again, caught her to his body, jerked up her face with a gesture of ruthless arrogance, and for the next few moments she was subjected to all the primitive demands of the pagan she had married. His mouth was hard and cruel, crushing her lips, bruising them as he forced them against her teeth. His body hard as steel itself, pressed to hers; she was almost fainting when at last he let her go.

Her sobs racked her slender frame. She

stared at him disbelievingly, as if she could not credit him with such unbridled passion, even though her bruises were there to prove it. She was angry still more so now because he had treated her so inhumanly. Words were whispered through her clenched teeth, words matching the blaze in her eyes.

'I hate you...hate you, do you hear?'

Paul looked at her across the room.

'This man,' he rasped, ignoring her words, 'You picked him up, you say?'

She had no further wish to talk about Bill. What she had endured at the hands of her irate husband was more than enough to be going on with.

'Let it drop,' she said, turning to take possession of a chair, which she thankfully sank into, for her legs were still weak.

'By God, we shall not let it drop! He was English, you say? And you took him to lunch at—' He broke off, crimson lines of fury creeping up the sides of his jaw. 'Took him to lunch with your aunt and uncle! What did you tell them? You must have given some excuse for picking up this man—'

'It wasn't picking up,' she protested. It had never for one moment seemed like that. She had at first felt it was not quite right to be talking to a stranger, but she now realised that it was fear of what Paul would say rather than a feeling of self-guilt at doing something wrong. 'We spoke to one another, and from that it led to our chatting, and his asking if—if I'd had my lunch—'

'So you said no, and eagerly asked him to lunch at your uncle's hotel!' His wrath had not abated one scrap. In fact, Tina was expecting another demonstration of it at any moment, since his hands were opening and closing in little spasmodic jerks, as if they were itching to inflict more pain on her already aching body.

'Paul,' she quivered, prudently deciding to adopt a more docile attitude in the hope that his temper would abate, 'please don't talk about it. There was nothing wrong—'

'Nothing wrong in picking up!' he broke in thunderously. 'If you were a Greek girl you'd be flogged for such wanton behaviour!'

'I'm not a Greek,' she submitted quietly.

'You're married to a Greek, and by God, you'll conform to the demand we put on our women!'

Her temper flared despite her resolve to practise caution.

'I'm English!' she flashed, 'and I'm not obliged to conform to such stupid, outdated customs! You said yourself that *my* ideals were outdated—you appear to have forgotten that!'

'We're not talking about your ideals, but about my rights as a husband. I have a right to punish you if in my opinion you have done wrong.' His voice was quieter now but still dangerously threatening. 'In Greece the husband is the master, and his word is obeyed.' He looked directly at her. 'You, Tina, will obey my wishes, or else suffer the consequences.'

'Wishes?' she repeated, stung to even greater anger by the implication of his words. That he would beat her seemed possible, and she thought how different he now was from the gentle, persuasive lover who had persistently endeavoured to win her as his pillow-friend. 'Orders, you mean!'

He inclined his head in a gesture of agreement.

'Orders, then. You'll obey them, Tina. In England the wife appears to wear the trousers; here, it is the husband. You knew that when you married me, didn't you?'

It was Tina's turn to incline her head. She said in muffled tones,

'Yes, I did know how it was with Greek men.'

'In that case you have no excuse for your conduct today. You knew it was something I would strongly object to. You have no complaint at the punishment I meted out to you just now—'

111

He stopped and wagged a finger at her, a gesture that infuriated her even more than the words that accompanied it. 'You were let off lightly. The next time I shall beat you.'

She swallowed the angry retort that leapt to her lips, saying instead,

'There was no harm in what I did. Bill—the young man—was not forward in any way—and, after all, I did take him to my uncle's hotel.'

The hard eyes glinted.

'Letting your relatives know there's something wrong between us.'

Tina's mouth moved convulsively. Spent as she was by Paul's rough handling of her, she wanted more than anything to be in his arms, to feel the strength of his body, his strong arms enfolding her. She said in soft and gentle tones,

'Paul...can we not talk any more about it? I'm—I'm s-so unhappy—' A great sob rising from the very depths of her heart put a sudden halt to her words, and she could only stare at him across the room, her eyes misty, her lovely face twisted as though reflecting some inner heartbreak. Paul seemed for a fleeting moment to remain hard and unemotional, and then, with a stride that was very different this time, he was close, bringing her up against him with the gentle insistence of his hand about her waist. She felt a leaden weight leave her body;

the bruises were nothing. She did not feel them any more as, with the infinite gentleness she had known before, her husband embraced her and kissed her, caressing her brow, her cheek, and presently bringing out a handkerchief to dry the tears of relief that had begun to fall.

'Tina,' he whispered, 'you do realise what started all this?'

'Yes—my—my foolishness in assuming that Dora had...' She trailed to silence, recalling the doubts her aunt had put into her head. She lifted her face to scan his eyes. Dark, unfathomable, pagan eyes that told her nothing. Could she believe him when he said that Dora had not slept with him? But if he had lied, then was it any of her business? It had happened before his marriage...She was well aware that she took the easy way out when she argued with herself like this, but all she wanted at this moment was to have her husband back the way he was before the intrusion of his old flame into their lives last evening.

He did wait a while for her to finish the sentence, but spoke eventually as he realised she had nothing more to say.

'It was unfortunate that she called, Tina. Once, a long time ago, we were rather more than friends. I've already mentioned this, I believe. I might have married her—I can't say.

113

It doesn't matter any more; I'm satisfied with my wife and would not change her for a dozen Doras—' He stopped and a hint of amusement took away the last vestige of harshness from his features. 'You look happier, my dear,' he observed finally.

'I am happier—when you say a thing like that to me.'

She shone up at him, that terrifying scene forgotten. Forgotten too was her resolve to act as if she did not care any more. He knew she loved him and she strongly suspected it would take far more effort than she could produce to convince him that she had changed.

'Don't goad me, Tina,' he said, and it did seem that there was the hint of a plea in his voice. 'My temper is something I'd far rather you did not see. The very idea of your spending the day with another man caused me to see red.' He held her from him and she saw that some of the sternness had come into his face again. She clung to him in tenderness, hoping to convince him that she had intended no wrong. The thought swiftly passed through her brain that she had arranged to meet Bill tomorrow, but she was soon dismissing it, deciding to meet him briefly and make some excuse for leaving him again within minutes. 'I am sure, Tina, that I gave you some hint that I'd make

114

a very jealous husband.'

She nodded, but said nothing. For she was thinking that it was always said that there could be no jealousy without love. This was obviously not true. Paul did not love her, but undoubtedly he could be jealous. His pagan jealousy had led him to sheer unbridled cruelty, and even if he was sorry now that was no guarantee that he would not do the same again, should she be so unwise as to give him cause.

She felt the thrill of his lips, the tenderness of his hand on her throat, her brow, her hair. After a long while he held her from him and said,

'Get yourself dolled up and we'll go out to dine.'

Her world was rosy again! Her feet seemed to be on air as she went from him to the room in which she had slept last night. She bathed, then came into the bedroom to find him there. He had showered and was in a dressing gown, red and black with dragons embroidered into it.

'What shall I wear?' she asked. The towel was all she had on; it was wrapped around her and tucked in under her armpits. 'The white satin-velvet which you bought me in Dorchester?'

He nodded absently, his eyes probing the folds of the bath sheet to what lay seductively beneath. Tina blushed and lowered her eyes demurely. She knew he was tempted; what she did not know was just how beautiful and alluring she looked to this dark and amorous Greek who was her husband. He was seeing the contours of her slender figure, mentally caressing them. His eyes moved to take in the fresh bloom of her cheeks, the soft full lips parted in a smile, the cascade of golden hair with its threads that here and there looked like silver, caught as they were in the light from the lamp. His eyes shifted fractionally to her wide forehead, then to the arched eyebrows and finally to her beautiful eyes, shaded by incredibly long lashes, curling and dark. His voice was a throaty bass tone when at last he spoke.

'You have no right to look so ravishing as this at such an early hour, Tina. Shall we go out or shall we stay in?'

'I—I...' She turned shyly from him, but his hand was there, taking hold of hers, drawing her to him. And the towel was untucked with a swift deft flick of his fingers and as it dropped to the floor Tina was brought to him, aware that his dressing gown had come open...and that he had nothing on beneath it. Their bodies touched, firing Tina with ecstasy. Paul wrapped his arms about her, his hands roving, his mouth forcefully demanding, hurting, but in the most exciting way.

'God, Tina! No woman has drawn me as you have—no, never in my life!' The vortex of his passion was released, carrying her with it as he melted her body to his. For a dizzy moment her brain whirled and it seemed that her breath had stopped. The room seemed to be spinning as her husband swept her up into his arms and moved with long impatient strides to the bed. The dressing-gown fell from him as he lay down beside her...It was a long time later that Paul said, his eyes on the gentle swell of her throat, his fingers caressing her breast,

'Shall we go out and eat, my Tina?' Amusement edged his voice and she laughed softly.

'It's the wrong way round, Paul.'

'Who cares? In any case, we can make love again when we come in.'

Her hand moved beneath the coverlet and she saw him close his eyes momentarily.

'I shall be too tired.' She pretended to yawn and received a slap for her trouble.

'Liar! In any case, I shall wake you up!'

She snuggled against him, her fingers pushing up, through the hair on his chest.

'Do you really want to go out?' she whispered.

'A man gets hungry,' he said.

'Come to think of it, I'm hungry too.'

'I thought you'd never admit it!'

She wore the white satin-velvet dress, gathered and pleated from the waist to give the skirt an exciting, glamorous fullness that swung outwards when she walked. The bodice was romantically cut low, an off-the-shoulder design of simple, unstudied elegance that showed off Tina's honey-peach skin and gave her a sophisticated air that seemed so very right for a night out in a plush restaurant in one of the city's most expensive hotels. A diamond clip ornamented her hair, matching the necklace and drop earrings which were Paul's wedding-present to her.

'You look beautiful,' whispered her husband close to her throat. 'How proud I am to take you out.'

She coloured faintly at the compliment, looking up into his eyes with a vital awareness of his charm. It seemed impossible that, only a few hours ago, his features had worn that satanic look, as hard and harsh as something cast in stone. Now, he wore an indulgent expression, half quizzical, half tender. And his lips were gentle on her own, his hands blissfully tender on the smooth bare flesh of her shoulder. He picked up the wrap lying there, on a chair, and lightly put it over her dress.

She took up her bag, gave him a slanting, winsome smile, and together they left the flat.

The moon was high above the golden city as they drove towards its centre; the Acropolis in all its ancient glory stood steeped in starlight, silent now, with only ghosts to roam the sacred precincts where once the goddess Athena held sway, contesting Poseidon for possession of Attica.

'Isn't it fascinating...?' Tina, sitting beside her husband as he drove the car, spoke softly, reverently, almost to herself. 'I think I'd have loved to live in the times of ancient Greece, when the gods of Olympus held sway.'

He laughed quietly, slanting her a glance and then swiftly returning his attention to the road.

'Why would you have loved to live at that time?'

'For one thing, I'd have known all about the gods. I know so little, even though I've read a great deal about Greek mythology.'

'You'd have been just as confused as you are today.'

'Perhaps you're right. The books one reads make it sound so real, so true—about the gods, I mean, and it's baffling to separate fact from fiction.' She paused a moment, but Paul was absorbed with the traffic, which was growing heavier now that the centre of the city was being approached. 'Athena was an enigma—good one moment and bad the next.'

'Never bad, vengeful, I admit—'

'Vengeance is always bad,' argued his wife. 'It means that people are harbouring a grudge.'

Again a slanting glance came her way.

'Don't you ever bear a grudge against anyone?' he enquired curiously.

'I try not to...' answered his wife meditatively. 'No, I don't believe I've ever borne a grudge against anyone, Paul.'

He shrugged but made no comment, and in any case, he was very soon drawing into the short drive of the most expensive hotel in the city. He had booked a table only an hour or so earlier, by telephone, but it was one of the best in the restaurant that was reserved for them. The waiter knew Paul, and treated him with a deference amounting almost to servitude. The table was by the window, so that the bustling panorama of the city could be seen, with the temples of the Acropolis etched in clear-cut silhouette against the Grecian sky. Tina gave a contented little sigh which brought a smile to her husband's olive-skinned face.

'That sounds like the cosy purr of a pussy who is being stroked,' he said quizzically. She laughed and asked what he meant by a 'cosy' purr.

'I've never heard the expression before,' she added.

'It ought to be self-explanatory—' He broke off as the waiter appeared with the wine list. 'Excuse me, my dear, while I peruse this carefully. Tonight calls for something special.'

'Special?' she repeated when the waiter had gone. 'What's so special about this evening?'

'Our first quarrel—and the glorious making up—You blush adorably, by the way—' He was watching her quizzically from above the embroidered cover of the wine list. 'Have I ever told you before?'

She said, marvelling at the cool practicality of her voice,

'Choose the wine, Paul, the waiter is only just there—' She flicked a finger indicatively. 'He's expecting to be called over and all you're doing is remarking on my appearance.'

The dark metallic eyes glittered, but only teasingly.

'Remind me to give you a clip over the ear when we get home—for impertinence!'

A laugh escaped her, and then there was silence while Paul chose the wine. Tina watched his face, profoundly conscious, as always of his attractions—those alert, dark eyes, all-seeing at times, pagan-hard at others, the clear brown skin tightly stretched over high classical cheekbones, the straight nose so typical of the Greek statues, the mouth with its full, sensuous lips, the formidable jawline and thrusting chin, both of which spelt mastery not unmingled with arrogance. A truly impressive face, matching the superlative quality of his physique and his innate air of nobility. How had she won such a man for her husband? Involuntarily a sigh resulted from the question, because the answer in all its stark truth and reality was there as well: she had him for her husband only because she had refused to be his pillow-friend.

CHAPTER SIX

The island of Patmos came into view through a mist of rain, gradually taking shape as the yacht glided gracefully towards the tiny port of Skala.

Paul's mother lived in one of the ancient houses of Chora—a beautiful house with arches and balconies and terraced gardens where scarlet hibiscus vied in splendour with bougainvillaeas and vivid crimson poinsettias. Although late in the year these flowers still bloomed, the gardens being well sheltered by thick cypress hedges and laurels. Tall pines grew up the hillsides to the east and north, while in another direction the houses extended right up to the towering eleventh-century monastery dedicated to St John the Apostle who, in a grotto close by, received the revelation and wrote the Apocalypse.

The rain had stopped by the time Tina and her husband arrived at his mother's house. The sun was quickly drying up the moisture on flowers and paths, but the earth smelled delightfully fresh and the pillars and steps had the clean bright look of newly washed marble.

'What a beautiful place!' breathed Tina, hoping her mother-in law would prove to be a fitting person to have possession of such a delightful home. Paul had told Tina that his aunt had been taken to hospital the week before and would not be coming out yet awhile.

'So you will not be meeting Aunt Sophia,' he said.

Tina privately felt that perhaps one of his relatives would be enough at a time. Paul had told her that his aunt spoke no English at all and his mother very little.

The old lady was seated in an arched saloon, austerely furnished with a ponderous dresser and table with matching chairs, an upholstered suite in dark green velvet and a high sideboard along the back of which stood a row of ancient ikons, the paintwork cracked to the point of sheer unsightliness. Two small candles burned at each end of these ikons, their flames throwing an almost eerie light on the ikons nearest to them. Tina extended a hand to her mother-in-law, feeling more strange than at any time since her marriage. For here was the real Greek home, its occupant an old lady dressed entirely in black, her gown touching the floor. Her face was wrinkled, her cheeks sunken to such an extent that the bones above them protruded, shining through the dull parchment of her skin. Her eyes alone seemed alive, alert, and they held within their dark depths all the pagan arrogance that Tina had seen in those of her son. Tina tried to imagine her as a young girl, but it was impossible. Mrs Christos was one of those women who seemed to have been old all their lives.

'*Xerete,*' murmured the old woman through parched lips which were no more than a thin slit in her face. '*Ti kanete?*' The merest pause and then, '*Me enoite?*'

Tina looked at her husband bewilderedly.

'Mother greeted you,' he said. 'And then she asked how you were. Lastly she wanted to know if you understood her.' He turned to his mother, a smile on his lips. 'You can speak in English, surely, my *mitera?*'

The hard eyes were unmoving as his mother replied, in Greek, bringing a frown to her son's dark face. Tina with swift perception drew her own conclusions: Mrs Christos did not approve of her son's marriage and therefore she was not intending to speak her language—not one single word of it!

Paul spread his hands and looked apologetically at his wife.

'Say something in English, Tina, and I'll

translate it.' He went on to say that if Tina spoke slowly his mother would probably be able to understand what she was saying. Tina nodded and said,

'I'm happy to meet you, Mrs—er...' She stopped, painfully conscious of a feeling of total inferiority.

'My *mitera*,' submitted Paul. 'You must address her as your mother.'

Tina frowned but lowered her head so that neither her husband or his mother should see. She tried again, saying this time,

'It's a pleasure to meet you, my *mitera*. I hope you are well.'

Paul translated what she had said. Tina watched closely waiting for some sign that the woman had understood in the first place, but it was impossible to draw anything from those black unmoving eyes, sunken into their sockets and yet as bright and piercing as those of her son.

She said quietly,

'*Ime kala, efaristo.*'

There was no need for a translation of this. Tina had learned enough Greek to know that Mrs Christos had said she was well, and to add a 'thank you' at the end.

The eyes were as still as ever and yet Tina felt the sensitive prickle of nerves at being throughly examined...and found wanting. She wished she had not worn a dress which was so low-cut and sleeveless. She wished it was a little longer. But Paul had chosen it, and it was to please him that she had it on now. He had an authoritative way with him when his wife was dressing, and would tell her imperiously what to wear. She obeyed meekly, not only because it was more comfortable to obey her husband, but also because he possessed a flair for knowing just what she would look best in for any particular occasion. Yet she could not help feeling that he had made a mistake this time. He should have known that his mother, being so old-fashioned herself, would look with considerable disfavour on the dress which her daughter-in-law was wearing.

Refreshments were brought by a middle-aged Greek woman wearing black, her hair wispy and grey and dressed in two thin plaits which went down her back, their ends fastened together with a piece of black string that looked like a bootlace. She brought black walnuts that had been pickled in a thick syrup so that their hard shells had become soft and edible. A glass of water accompanied each dish of these walnuts, which were taken up singly on a long fork, dipped in the water, and then eaten. Tina, never having seen them before, simply watched her husband and followed what he did, aware of his half-amused expression at her hesitance. Coffee followed, then some sticky confections which Paul declined, flicking a hand when the woman servant offered them to him.

Tina, fascinated by the room, allowed her eyes to wander all around it. There was a whole conglomeration of bric-à-brac on the dresser but some lovely antique plates as well. The pictures on the walls seemed valuable, and so did the various silver objects lying around. But there was no doubt that this aspect was poverty-stricken in comparison to the luxury of Paul's villa, his flat and his yacht. He told her later that his mother had refused to take any of her husband's money when he died; she had sold up her own home and gone to live with her sister. However, her sister's house caught fire one day and was burned down. This lovely old house had been bought with the money Mrs Christos had got from the sale of her house, but, Tina gathered, there had been some help from Paul—limited help, as it was obvious that his mother was far too proud to accept very much at all.

'It seems—frugal,' was Tina's reply when, in their bedroom, they had the chance to talk in private. 'Not at all what I expected.

The house is beautiful, of course, but the furnishings...'

'It's what these old people are used to, Tina. They care nothing for anything that isn't a necessity. For instance, it would be impossible for me to persuade Mother to dine out with us. On her rare visits to Athens she is most uncomfortable in the flat—and even worse in the villa.'

Tina could believe that. She supposed that Mrs Christos would feel exceedingly strange and out of place in one of the plush hotels where Paul took his wife to dine.

'Has she been on your yacht?' she asked curiously. Paul laughed and shook his head.

'No, never.'

'But she does visit Athens?'

'Very occasionally. She comes by boat, but the boats they use are much larger than the yacht.'

'She never flies?'

'You would never get my mother on an aeroplane—unless it was by force, and I suspect that even then you'd have a struggle.'

Tina fell silent for a while before saying, rather hesitantly,

'She doesn't like me, Paul.'

He seemed to heave a litle sigh.

'As I explained, she has this grudge against

the English. It's something I have tried to shake her out of, but it isn't any use. However, she'll get used to you, my dear. Don't take it to heart, will you?'

She smiled and shook her head.

'Of course I won't, Paul. I must admit that after what you said I wasn't expecting her to receive me with open arms.'

'I'm sorry, my dear,' he said, then let the matter drop, changing the subject as he told her he would take her to the Grotto of the Apocalypse on the following day. 'This is the most sacred island in the Aegean,' he added, but perhaps you already knew this?'

She shook her head.

'I thought Delos was the most sacred island,' she returned, puzzled.

'In antiquity it was Delos. I am speaking about today.'

'Oh, I see. It's because of St John the Apostle, I suppose?'

'That's right. Many pilgrims come to the Grotto every year.'

Tina was naturally looking forward to the visit, but, meanwhile, there was the evening to get through and she had the strong premonition that it would prove to be an ordeal. And she was right. Mrs Christos would not speak English, so her son was forced to translate everything. Tina tried to be sociable, to smile, to draw the woman out a little, but she was aloof, distantly hostile, sitting erect in her high-backed chair, like a statue of one of the Greek goddesses. Formidable she appeared, with her gnarled hands always clasped in front of her, those eyes unmoving but holding such secrets in their depths. Her frame was thin and bony, her hair enclosed in a coif that allowed only a few silver threads to escape. Even when she was at the table, eating her evening meal, she was silently aloof, unfriendly. It seemed to Tina that she was not even glad to see her son.

Tina went off on her own after dinner, feeling she must escape for a while, and of course it would give mother and son the chance of some private conversation.

The air was chill but not uncomfortably so, and Tina wandered right through the grounds and entered the lane beyond. The sea lay below, caressed by starlight, slumbering beneath an endless canopy of purple sky. The monastery walls, knife-edged and moon-tinted, seemed to possess a rare and haunting beauty that gave the impression of eternal peace, and a grandeur that was as simple as it was profound. She could imagine the hermit who, coming here, had erected the lovely monastery to the memory of St John. His name was St

Christodoulos, a pious man who received the island as a gift from the Byzantine Emperor Alesius Comnenus almost nine hundred years ago.

She wandered on, her interest moving alternately from the shadowed carob slopes to the sea, then to the mountainous masses of volcanic origin, not very high, but impressively awesome for all that. On the sea the moonlight caressing the waves caused a quivering pulsation of light over the water; in the great dome of the heavens above it a million stars held their trembling, precarious positions in the vast space that was infinity. Tina, affected in some indefinable way, felt small and insignificant, a mere speck of dust in the universe. Depression descended on her like a heavy blanket and she turned, frowning and a trifle angry that her mind was affected in this way. Life was good; she had a wonderful husband, a lovely home... so why should she be depressed? Perhaps it was the silence, and the loneliness, because she was on her own, out here, where magic and romance ought by rights to be a mere breath away.

She was missing her husband. She wanted him with her, holding her hand, stopping now and then to kiss her, to caress her with all the confidence that the rights of a husband gave him.

She turned about, retracing her steps towards the high wrought-iron gate through which she had come. The cypresses and palms and lemon trees surrounding the grounds of the house made strange, ill-defined shapes in the moonlight; the monastery looked far away, remotely unapproachable. She entered through the gates, and advanced towards the house, her steps slow, her mind a little confused. For although she had returned she had no desire to enter the house. Mrs Christos repelled her, with her unfathomable gaze, her sparse, erect body clothed in black, her thin mouth and claw-like hands. It seemed impossible that she had brought a child into the world who would grow into a man as handsome as Paul.

As she approached the house Tina saw that a window was open, and the light streaming through on to the lawn. Perhaps she could go in through that window, she thought, unable to see from this distance whether it was a french window or not. She presently discovered it was not and continued past it. Then she stopped suddenly, involuntarily, because the voice she heard was pitched in anger. The one answering was quiet but firm. Paul was speaking in Greek, just as his mother had done. They were quarrelling, the woman's anger manifest in her raised voice, Paul's in the low vibration which infiltrated now and then into the more steady and firm inflections. Tina frowned, her instinct telling her that she herself was the reason for this quarrel. And then, as she stood there, she heard the word which she could separate from all the others. Dora...

It came again, spoken this time by Paul. More words in Greek, more anger expressed by the woman, and then the name again.

Dora.

Without any doubt at all Tina knew that Mrs Christos had wanted her son to marry Dora Vassilou.

It was the following morning that Tina found herself alone with her mother-in-law, Paul having gone to the yacht for something he had forgotten. Mrs Christos beckoned Tina, who was in the garden, waiting for her husband to return, when they were to go up to the Grotto. She went to the old woman, who was sitting by the open window.

'I want speak. You come to me!'

English! And not too bad at all!

'Is it important?' Tina wondered why her nerves were knotting up.

'Important—yes!'

'Very well.'

She went round to the front door and entered through the hall. Mrs Christos had moved from the window, to sit in the high-backed chair, erect, her hands clasped as they had been yesterday when her son and his wife had arrived.

'Sit—please.'

Tina obeyed, taking the chair indicated by the slight movement of the woman's head.

'What is it?' asked Tina, trying to be calm. She hated being alone with the woman; already she felt stifled, as if there were a great many people in the room instead of two.

'My son—why he marry you?' The hostility was not only in the voice but in the sudden twist of features already grotesque. Tina shivered involuntarily.

'There—there is usually only one reason for two people marrying,' she managed to say, uncaring that she was voicing what must be a white lie, indirectly of course.

'Pah! My son not love—He not—not able to love—not English girl! Greek girl he loves, but there is one time quarrel. Now this girl free—her man die!' Mrs Christos looked at her, the black eyes glinting with what could only be described as hatred. Tina, her face pale and her heart beating overrate, wanted to put her hands to her ears before she heard any more. Paul in

135

love with Dora…Was it true? It could be true. Dora had said that Paul had married her only to spite his old flame. 'He all time love this girl—this Dora Vassilou—This is her name before she marry—' Mrs Christos broke off, then said, looking questioningly at her daughter-in-law, *'Me enoite?'*

Tina nodded.

'Yes, I understand you.'

'Kala! You not know my Paul too long time before he marry you, *ne?* Yes?'

'Not too long,' answered Tina, glancing through the window, hoping her husband would come.

'He want to spite this nice Dora—good Greek girl who make good wife and have plenty sons—' Mrs Christos cast baleful eyes over Tina's slender figure. 'English girls—pah! They not want have many plenty sons for their mans—no!'

'I expect,' said Tina through whitened lips, 'that I shall eventually have children by my husband.' She spoke very slowly, stressing every word with clear enunciation. The woman sneered and almost spat out the words.

'No good strong sons from weak—weak—small *kore!'*

Tina coloured, and rose from the chair.

'I'm sorry if you are disappointed, Mrs

136

Christos,' she said coldly, 'but Paul has married me and it's too late to do anything about it—'

'Not too late!' flashed her mother-in-law wrathfully. 'I tell my Paul he must have of you the divorce! It is too easy in Greece—Priest give of the divorce for ten pounds gift to church! Ten pounds of English money—it is too easy!'

Tina had risen; she looked down into the sunken eyes and said quietly,

'I shall never agree to a divorce even if Paul should want one, Mrs Christos.' She found it impossible to address this woman as mother. She disliked her intensely and hoped her husband would never bring her here again. 'I will add—even though it disappoints you—that there is no danger of Paul's wanting to divorce me.' Not while she could hold him physically, she thought. But if ever the time should come when he tired of her...Marriage without love on his side...Well, she had known the risks, and had bravely taken them. What was her fate would surely come to her. And if it was her fate to be cast off then she would have no alternative than to accept it courageously and be thankful for the happiness she had already enjoyed.

'My Paul has never wanted to marry any girl but this nice Dora! It is because she is marrying other man that he angry—and now that other man die she can marry my son, but for you—! English slut!'

Tina stared at her, blinking. And then in a flash of perception she realised that the woman hadn't the smallest notion of what the word meant. So she forgave her, merely saying,

'Mrs Christos, I would not harbour any hope that Paul will want to divorce me. We are very happy together. I love him dearly and always shall love him.' Her voice was soft and sincere, but it made no impression on the woman sitting there, her eyes now turned towards the ikons, an intentness in their depths that was almost frightening. There was something unnatural about Paul's mother, and suddenly Tina was remembering where the family came from...Langadia; the inhabitants were called Anastenarides...the fire-dancers who kept alive a relic of ancient Dionysian worship...God of the vine who represented all that was irrational in man in contrast to the cult of Apollo, which was the worship of all that was good. 'If you will excuse me...?' Tina inclined her head in a gesture of respect and went towards the door. She turned as she reached it. Mrs Christos had risen and as Tina watched she went to the row of ikons and, starting at the left, began kissing them. Tina shuddered convulsively, her hand on the door knob. She turned it softly, opened the door, and went out.

What sort of a family had she married into? Paul on the surface was a cultured Greek, very Westernised in his ways, and in some of his outlooks on life. But what was he beneath the suave urbane veneer of polish? Would she be able to recognise the *real* man if ever he was revealed to her? Inevitably he must have much of his mother in him, for a mother passes many traits on to her sons, just as a father passes them on to his daughters. Regarded objectively, Mrs Christos was a pagan, despite the kissing of the ikons...and was not this kissing of the ikons paganism anyway?

Everything about her mother-in-law was vile to Tina, and she shuddered again as she went from the room, through the hall and into the clean pure air of the gardens. She saw Paul coming along the path, striding out with an easy swinging gait that brought his tall lean body closer and closer...For one wild uncontrolled moment she wanted to turn and run from him, from this son of the pagan woman she had just left. But she stood where she was, conscious of her pallor, of the trembling sensation within her that was affecting her heart, tying her nerves in hard little knots. Paul stopped a yard or so from her and stared, a frown bringing his brows together.

139

'Something wrong?' he asked, his voice expressing concern. 'Are you not feeling well, Tina?'

Her mouth was dry; fear was strong within her, fear of the unknown...yes, of the parts unknown of this man to whom she was married. She would never know how she managed to keep her voice level as she answered him.

'I'm feeling quite well, Paul. Did you find what you wanted?' she added, her eyes straying to the small box he held in his hand.

'Yes.' He stopped and lifted her face, for she had averted it without knowing why. She quivered at his touch, but now it was with a sort of reluctant revulsion rather than the sweet ecstasy which such a contact had previously given her. 'Something's upset you, child. What is it?'

She thought for one moment that she would tell him, but changed her mind, deciding it would do no good at all to make him angry with his mother.

'I'm not upset, Paul.' She feigned surprise and hoped it was effective in deceiving him. 'I don't know why you should say a thing like that.'

His frown deepened, then cleared, for she was smiling up at him, her hand on his. She had put it there with the intention of drawing

140

his away from her chin, but suddenly found that she dared not…in case she should arouse his anger. And so her hand remained on his, and he turned his own to take hers within it, curling his fingers in a way that should by right have thrilled her, but instead she knew another access of revulsion. She must have managed to hide it, though, because her husband's face retained its rather indulgent expression and his eyes were soft as they looked deeply into hers.

'Are you ready for our outing?' he wanted to know. 'I will just take this in to Mother and then I'll be with you.'

She stood stock still after he had gone, her mouth dry and her nerves still knotted into tight little balls. She had been looking forward to the visit to the Grotto, but now she would have done anything to avoid going there with her husband. She wanted to be on her own, to think, and think, to dwell on her foolishness in marrying in such haste. She had known practically nothing about the dark foreigner whom she was marrying.

'I'm afraid of him…' It was with wonderment mingling with her fear that the words escaped her. 'He's all right now, but how will he turn out when the novelty's worn off?' Would he be cruel? Would he remember that she loved him and make sure that he never hurt her? So many questions came to her mind, but the only effect they had was to tighten her knotted nerves, creating even more tension within her so that she felt she could scream, just for relief.

Paul came back into sight; she fell in beside him when he reached her and a short while later they were at the Grotto, having walked through a region of olive trees and carobs, where clean little flat-roofed villas nestled in gardens bright with flowers. A donkey brayed in a dusty field as they passed, a man with a dog and a little goat running alongside it raised a hand and said,

'*Kalimera!*' And Paul smiled and returned the greeting.

'*Kalimera!*'

A bearded priest came slowly, lifting his hand more lanquidly.

'*Kalimera!*'

'*Kalimera sas!*'

Tina looked up, puzzlement in her eyes.

'Why did you put *sas* on the end?' she wanted to know.

'It's a mark of respect when you speak to a priest,' he explained. 'It is usual to show this respect.' He spoke matter-of-factly, as if he had done this all his life. Tina was silent, dwelling on what she had been thinking about a short while ago. Paul a pagan...and yet he could extend this respect to a priest—and always had extended it.

The Grotto had been preserved. Paul told Tina that St John had lived there after being exiled by Domitian. Here he received the Apocalyptic visions, which he dictated to his disciple who took them all down.

In the depths of the Grotto was a step which, Paul said, served as St John's pillow.

'Just a tale,' said Paul with a smile. 'It couldn't possibly have served as a pillow.

After the Grotto they proceeded to the Monastery which, to Tina, was much more interesting with its beautiful frescoes on a background of gold, its ikons in silver and gold, its Treasury where there were crosses and mitres and chalices, and priceless manuscripts.

'Do you want to see the guest rooms?' asked Paul accommodatingly. Tina said yes, she would like that very much. It had always interested her that monastries provided for the casual visitor. She felt she would like to stay at one some day, but when she mentioned this to Paul he frowned and said,

'Not for me, Tina. I prefer the comfort of an hotel.'

He took her on to the terrace; it was a fresh clear morning and the view was magnificent with the island of Leros plainly to the south-east, the tiny islets of Arki and Lipsi to the east, and to the north the two horns of Cape Mycale, the isle of Samos—offshore of the coast of Asia Minor—and the mountainous island of Icaria.

'It's breathtaking!' Tina, feeling much more composed after savouring the quiet peace of the Monastery, spoke enthusiastically of the view. 'I've never seen anything like it!'

'It is a rather splendid view, I agree.'

'Do you come often to Patmos?'

'About four times a year.'

'Shall I have to come with you each time?' The scenery and the glorious view were forgotten; she was frowning at the idea of visiting her mother-in-law four times a year.

'Not if you'd rather not, my dear.'

She looked swiftly at him, astonished that he was being so considerate.

'She doesn't like me, you know.'

'In that case, Tina, you have no need to come again.'

'Never?' Strangely, it seemed sad that she and his mother had not taken to one another.

'It's entirely up to you. I shall ask you if you want to come, and the choice will be yours.'

'It's...kind of you,' she murmured, thinking that only a short time before she was troubled that one day he might be unkind to her.

'Not kind, Tina,' he corrected, 'merely sensible. If you and Mother haven't taken to one another then the obvious thing is for you not to meet.'

'It seems a shame, though.'

His glance had a curious quality about it.

'You sound as if you regret that it's turned out like this.'

'I do have regrets, yes, Paul. A girl wants to be liked by her husband's mother. It's natural. I shall feel shut out when you visit her.'

'Then don't,' he advised. 'I did tell you of Mother's aversion to the English. It is something she cannot overcome—perhaps she has no desire to overcome it. She is disappointed that I married an English girl, but she knows that I go my own way, that I please myself what I do. She's resigned but not at all happy about my marriage.'

Tina looked up at him.

'You're very frank about it,' she said.

'There's nothing to be gained by pretence. It was very plain to you that Mother did not mean the words of welcome with which she greeted you. As you gathered, she can speak a little English, but she was being stubborn and not intending to speak one word that you could understand.' He paused, but Tina said nothing. Her eyes had wandered, to the view

145

again, but her mind was on what had been said. 'I'm disappointed at her attitude but not surprised,' Paul was continuing. 'She and I have never been close; she's a strange lady, Tina, in that she has no need of others. She lives with my aunt for my aunt's sake, not for her own. She would be a lot happier if she were living entirely on her own.'

Tina looked distressed.

'It wouldn't do, Paul. She's old, and soon she won't be able to look after herself. How old is your aunt?'

'Seventy-six, four years older than Mother.'

'Oh...' The distress was in Tina's eyes again. 'Will she—I mean, is this illness serious?'

'Very. In fact it will surprise me if she gets better.'

'What will your mother do? Will she come to us?'

Paul glanced at her strangely.

'You wouldn't mind if she came to us?'

Tina hesitated; she couldn't help it.

'I suppose,' she said at length, 'that I'd get used to it. After all, she's your mother and I haven't the right to object—'

'But you have, Tina,' interrupted her husband quietly. 'It's your home as well as mine; it's your life which would be affected.'

'I don't think I could see her going into

146

a home,' she began.

Paul gave a little sigh, the only indication that he was troubled about his mother's future. He *was* troubled, though. Tina was sure of it, simply because all Greeks were concerned about the aged in their midst. There were no homes for old people; there was no call for such establishments as parents and grandparents were always tenderly cared for by their relatives.

'We shall just have to wait and see what happens to my aunt,' he said. 'In any case, Mother would probably refuse to come to us, and while she's able to take care of herself she would prefer to be on her own, as I have said.' He spoke with an edge of finality to his voice and Tina changed the subject, commenting again on the view, which had changed even while they stood there, on the terrace, for clouds had obscured the sun and everything seemed to have fallen into shadow. Over the sea a mist was rising, obscuring the horizon and the two white ships that had been gleaming in the sun just a short while ago.

'We'd better go back,' said Paul, taking her arm possessively. 'It's going to rain.'

Tina was thinking about his mother as they made their way back to the house. She wondered what Paul would have to say if she told him of his mother's open antagonism towards her. That he would be angry went without saying, but what really interested Tina was whether or not she would learn—either from his expression or his manner—if he had in fact married her to spite his old flame. However, as she had no intention of relating to him what had taken place between his mother and herself in his absence, it was profitless to speculate, and she managed to dismiss the matter entirely from her mind. She dearly loved her husband and she meant to grasp what happiness she could. The future might bring heartache—she felt instinctively that it would, because for one thing her fear of Paul a short while ago had been very real and she firmly believed that her fear would return, over and over again—but this was the present and she intended to take all that it offered. As always, she was philosophic about life and fate, believing that one's destiny was mapped out at birth. Whatever was in store for her must come. It was inevitable and therefore it had to be accepted.

She felt her husband's hand taking hers and every other thought was erased by the little access of sheer undiluted pleasure that spread through her. She glanced up at his firm, arresting profile and her love for him filled her whole being. Life was good!

He turned, to slant her a glance; she gave him a smile, and he responded. There was no one about and the olive groves were darker than before, with dark clouds pressing lower in a wide expanse of threatening rain. She said softly.

'Kiss me, Paul,' and although he gave a light, surprised little laugh, he stopped, caught her to him, and claimed her eager lips in a long and tender kiss.

CHAPTER SEVEN

Three days later they were back in Crete, and for a fortnight life ran smoothly, with Paul at home the whole time as he was able, he said, to do his work here, in the spacious study that was built away from the villa, in the grounds where it had its own small garden surrounded by hedges and trees. It was totally private and secluded and Tina had never ventured anywhere near when Paul was working there. He had shown it to her, naturally, and she had stood, a trifle dazed by the luxurious décor and furniture, the number of books, the priceless paintings on the walls. The desk was massive, an antique beautifully inlaid with brass; the carpet was like down to the feet; it was of a colour between blue and green and matched the long drapes that framed two enormous windows. Gay sunblinds had been fitted over these windows on the outside and in addition there were the shutters which were fixed to all the windows. In most houses these had to be closed in the real heat of the summer, shutting out all light as well as the heat. But of course the whole of the villa property was air-conditioned, eliminating the heat problem altogether. One long wall of the study was lined with shelves, everyone of which was filled to capacity with books.

'What a pleasant place to work in,' she had said. 'It's no wonder you love being out here. I'd be just the same myself. I don't think I'd ever want to go to Athens at all.'

He had smiled and reminded her that if he had not been in Athens at one particular time he and she would never have met.

It seemed a long time ago, she was thinking now, as she wandered close to Paul's study and stood by the gate, looking into the garden. The study building was hidden from sight owing to a curve in the path, but suddenly Paul appeared, stopping momentarily as he saw her there. She coloured a little as he came towards her, his eyes taking on a quizzical expression.

'Looking for someone?' he teased, taking her hand as he reached her.

'I was just taking a stroll,' she murmured.

'Are you lonely?' he wanted to know. She shook her head.

'Of course not. I don't know why I stopped there; it wasn't because I was feeling lonely or bored.'

151

'I'm finished for today,' he said, delighting her by the news. 'We'll have an early lunch and go to Knossos.'

'That'll be lovely!' They had been once, not long after their marriage, but there were crowds of tourists about at that time and Paul had promised to bring her later in the year, when they would have the site practically to themselves.

They lunched on *barbouni* with *paidhakya* as a second course, washed down with *retsina*. The dessert was fresh fruit—oranges and apples and *karpouzi*.

The drive to the Palace of Knossos was as usual one of tremendous interest to Tina, who even now found something intriguing in the Cretan way of life. She still could stare at the spectacle of black-robed women shepherding goats and sheep—their bells making music as they tinkled through the air—to and from the pastures. Other women would be leading donkeys laden with logs or vegetables or some other load which always seemed too heavy for the poor, persecuted animals to endure. Some women were in the fields gathering kindling for their fires and outdoor ovens, others were carrying pails of milk home to their families. And while all these chores were being undertaken by the women their menfolk were sprawling in cafés, cigarettes between their lips, their hands busy with their *komboloi*—strings of worry beads that were treated rather like rosaries. Tina said, speaking her thoughts aloud,

'In Greece only the men worry, it seems. Women probably never have the time.'

Paul flicked her a quizzical glance and said with a hint of sardonic amusement,

'Sarcasm, eh? The women here are happier than you think.'

'I can't believe they are.'

'They've never known anything different.'

'The older ones, perhaps. The young girls aren't fools. They know about the West, and that we aren't treated in that way by our menfolk.'

'A woman is far happier if she has a master,' he said with a confidence that vexed his wife into saying,

'How do you know? You assume too much, Paul—you and all the rest of the Greek men!'

He looked at her, taking his eyes off the road for a second.

'Can you honestly say that you aren't happy now that you've got yourself a master?' So casual the tone! Tina's vexation increased to real annoyance.

'I don't regard you as my master,' she informed him stiffly.

'Then you should, because I am just that.' His tone was still casual, matter-of-fact. 'Nature decreed that the male of the species should be dominant—'

'Rubbish! In the animal world perhaps! But we happen to have risen above the stage of being animals.'

Paul raised his eyebrows fractionally.

'If we aren't animals, then what are we?' he demanded.

'You know what I mean! We're animals—all right, I agree! But we're the higher animals and we've progressed far beyond the stage where the male was dominant.'

He did not speak and a silence fell for a few moments. Tina, controlling her temper with difficulty, turned from his taut formidable profile and looked out of her side window. They were passing through another village and there was an arcade of small shops, all with their doors wide open. In one a barber was shaving a youth, while his assistant was standing watching him. In a *taverna* a dark Greek was bending over a charcoal grill, cooking *souvlaki*, and from another *taverna* close by *bouzouki* music was being relayed on a tape recorder and a man could be seen leaping and gyrating as he threw himself into one of the Greek dances. His clothes were voluminous and Tina wondered

154

if he carried a knife in them. It had been a matter of incredulity that the Cretan men carried knives, ready to defend themselves or perhaps attack an enemy. Wild, they were, but at least Paul had no Cretan blood in his veins...or so he had told her.

Paul spoke at last, breaking what had been an uncomfortable silence. He told her that the vineyards through which they were now passing belonged to him. These were extensive, and men could be seen working on the terraces. Olive groves came next; these were also his property, he said.

'The vineyards are a legacy,' he explained. I don't trade in wine; the grapes are sold to a merchant.'

Shipping and olive-cultivation were his business, but it seemed that he had a hand in various other things. He owned an hotel on the island of Chios, she had discovered, and another on the island of Skiathos.

'This is the Knossos Valley,' he was telling her a few moments later. 'It's one of the most fertile valleys in the whole of Greece.'

She saw it from a different approach from that of her first visit, but it was equally attractive. She recalled that the Palace had lain beneath a hill on which grew grapes and olives. And then one day a man ploughing his land close by brought to light some vases. The Turks were rulers of the island at that time and refused to have the region excavated, but once they were ejected and the Cretans gained their independence the English archaeologist Sir Arthur Evans was permitted to excavate. Although only an amateur he was willing to spend a quarter of a million pounds of his own money on the project, so convinced was he that a great treasure lay buried beneath the mound.

It turned out to be one of the most incredible discoveries of the world, and a boon to the island's economy, since the Palace of King Minos at Knossos brought thousands of tourists to Crete every year. For Tina, it was the most wonderful excavation of any she had seen. Delphi was dramatic in its setting, but of its treasures there was little left. In Crete, the Palace—originally reputed to contain over eight hundred rooms—had been restored by Evans, and even the frescoes had been left where they were originally. The actual throne of Minos was there, for any tourist to sit upon!

In spite of the lateness of the season there were one or two groups, escorted by their guides, and Paul gave a wry grimace as he said,

'Just the same as the Acropolis of Athens—almost impossible to get it to oneself.'

'Never mind; I'm happy to be here. And

there aren't anywhere near the number of people we saw when we came before.'

The guide was talking. She was a small, middle-aged woman with dark hair and eyes; she wore a black skirt and a light blue sweater under a camel coat which was open, for the day was warm and sunny, although the heights of Mount Ida were hidden in a layer of cloud. The guide was saying that the first Minoan palace was built about the year two thousand B.C. and rebuilt several times before its final destruction six hundred years later.

'Let us move away,' suggested Paul putting his hand beneath his wife's elbow. 'I can tell you all you want to know about it.'

They had entered by way of a procession corridor; on the wall was a lovely fresco showing hundreds of people before a white-robed goddess. The original of the fresco, Paul said, was in the museum.

'So this is only a copy?'

He nodded.

'That's right. Some of the originals have been left intact, but it's better, in the main, to remove treasures and put them into a museum.'

'It's certainly safer, and a lot more people can see them, of course.'

'You will find, when we go to the museum, that these Minoan people were much smaller than the Cretans of today,' he added.

'*Much* smaller?'

'Yes; their graves are no larger than a child's.'

'That's interesting. So I expect the finds in the tombs are small, too.'

'Of course. Some of the statues are no more than six or eight inches high.'

'It must have made the excavations difficult?'

'It certainly did. However, Evans was a much more gentle excavator than, say, Schliemann, who dug as if he were trenching his back garden. Sir Arthur Evans loved his work here and spent thirty years of his life on it.'

Tina nodded, remembering that his heart was buried here, at Knossos, the place he loved above anywhere else on earth.

'He must have been a wonderful man,' she said, almost reverently, 'to have given so much of his life, and his money, to this project.'

'But what a fulfilment! Schliemann wanted to excavate, and many people believe it was a fortunate circumstance that the Turks refused him permission to do so.'

'He'd have ruined many of the treasures?'

'Very likely. He had no finesse as an archaeologist. His wife, now—she was very different. She would use a minute brush where he would wield a spade.'

'Women are gentler,' she mused, not meaning it in the way her husband took it.

'Putting us men down again, are you?'

'I didn't mean it quite like that,' she said, laughing. 'You're in a mood to take offence for the least thing today, Paul.'

'No such thing. You, my child, are in a waspish mood.'

'Tell me some more about the excavations,' she invited, determined not to clash with him. They had left the corridor and were in a central courtyard which was flooded by a tide of brilliant colour enhanced by the soft yellow beams of sunlight as they slanted on to the brightly-frescoed walls, the red and black columns, the huge earthenware jars of soft red ochre, the scintillating stars that were in reality mica in the stones forming the floor on which they were standing. An Arabic-jasmine vine tumbled in enchanting disorder over the stones, a few bright blue blossoms still flaunted their colour among the delicately-shaped green leaves.

Paul began to talk, his voice low, attractive as always to Tina's sensitive ears; she loved the accent, the cultured intonation, the clear yet quiet inflections when a word here and there was stressed. He told her that the term Minoan was used to define the Copper and Bronze Ages in Crete, and he went on to talk about the Palace, and the great difficulties experienced when succeeding floor levels had to be preserved.

'Not only preserved,' he went on, 'but disentangled. 'It's always the upper floors, excavated first, that present difficulties. Here at Knossos, where there are so many storeys, they had to roof in various parts of the Palace, to put back into place such things as door-jambs, column bases and paving stones that had fallen down from one floor to the one below.'

'It must have been a colossal job,' she said, awed.

'Look how long it took. There were others who came after Evans.'

'And hundreds of men must have been working here.' She had moved on, with Paul beside her. Her eyes wandered to walls painted with flowers and fish and birds. Wasp-waisted princes and princesses were adorned with necklaces of lilies, their hair delicately styled into long black curling locks. Round their waists they wore metal girdles; above their waists they were naked, below they wore a kind of kilt, very short, revealing beautiful limbs. On their wrists they wore beautiful seal-stones, minutely engraved.

'I've seen something like this in Egyptian

illustrations,' said Tina musingly.

'There was a lot of coming and going between the Minoans and the Egyptians,' explained Paul. 'These princes and princesses do bear a most striking resemblance to the "Great Ones of Keftiu" whom you can see on Egyptian tombs. They were bringing gifts from Minos to Pharaoh.'

They continued, talking and strolling, moving away from the groups of tourists as they occasionally caught up with them.

Descending to lower chambers, they walked along a maze of corridors and Tina could well imagine that this vast edifice had been identified with the famous labyrinth where Theseus would have been lost had it not been for the help of Ariadne, the beautiful princess who fell in love with him. In King Minos's throne room was the chair, made of alabaster, which was his throne. Tina watched as one or two people sat on it, all looking sheepish but determined to go home able to say they had sat on the throne of the ancient King.

'Aren't you going to sit on it?' asked Paul teasingly, and Tina shook her head at once.

'No, thank you. I never make a fool of myself if I can help it,' she laughed.

Later they came to the Queen's apartment and Tina was told of the excellent plumbing facilities. There were baths and toilets—flush toilets—and even septic tanks for drainage.

'They were concerned with hygiene, obviously,' she observed.

'They were noted for their cleanliness.'

'I wonder where they are now?'

'Dead and gone,' answered her husband, laughing.

'You know what I meant. Their descendants. Where are they now?'

'Some of them are here, I expect. It was a long time ago, you know,' he reminded her.

'The present-day Cretans are often tall,' she pointed out. 'The Minoans were small, you said.'

'Other tribes would infiltrate,' he explained. 'Every race is a mixture of many other races; you must know that.'

She fell silent, and for the next quarter of an hour or so they just wandered about, hand in hand, content just to be together in this incredible setting, this House of the Double Axe as it was called.

At last they left the Palace, taking a quiet lane that once had been the main road of what was at that time a busy city. It was a narrow lane, and Tina recalled that horses came late to Crete. The usual form of transport for the rich was by palanquin, carried by slaves, whose bare feet had trodden the very same stones over which Tina and Paul were now walking.

'So long ago,' she whispered. 'Long, long before the birth of Christ this marvellous civilisation flourished. We think of cave-men and total lack of culture...' She shook her head and again lapsed into silence.

'You have to remember,' Paul said, 'that here in Greece a highly-developed culture existed when other parts of the world were not even emerging from the primordial shadows of total ignorance.'

She nodded, still carried away by the wonder of it all. She felt she would like to go back, just for a day, so that she could see what these people were like, how they lived, ate, slept.

It was five o'clock when they got back to the car. Tina stood watching an eagle weaving patterns of his flight, and then in total contrast her eyes were caught by a long green lizard darting about along the rock wall by which the car was parked. It was trying to catch a crawling insect, but swift though its movements were the insect appeared quite able to dodge its dangerous forked tongue. Tina smiled when at last the lizard gave up and sat, stock still, its head right up, its eyes unmoving.

She heard Paul say with a hint of amusement, 'That one escaped, my dear, but only to bring another to its death. The lizard must eat.'

She sighed and turned, to get into the car. He closed the door and went round to his own side.

'A *taverna* for afternoon tea,' he decided. 'I know just the place.'

It was away off the road, a pretty villa in a lemon orchard. The young couple who kept it had been married less than a year. The villa was Leda's dowry along with some money and ten goats. The couple had succumbed to an arranged marriage but were fortunate enough to have fallen in love on sight. Leda was slender and fair. Of true Doric stock, she had preserved her racial purity and her husband, a dark Cretan from the north of the island, was tremendously proud of her. She spoke English, an asset when she and Costalis decided that as they had not very much land they would open a café, using the one big hall of the villa, the sitting-room, and the large patio. They had done so well during this first year that they were already thinking of extending the villa.

Leda greeted Tina with a rose, and the words,

'Welcome to our *cafenion*, Mrs Paul. We hear that you are marry, Mr Paul.'

He smiled at her and said jokingly,

'Yes, Leda. My bachelor days are over.'

'It is good,' from Costalis wisely. 'Many big sons come now.'

Tina coloured and sighed at the same time. It would seem that she ought by now to be expecting a child. Yet Leda had not yet produced one, nor was she likely to do so in the immediate future.

She and Costalis were busy behind the scenes; she could hear them chattering in Greek, hear cutlery clattering and crockery being bounced on to a tray. The Greeks never did anything quietly, she had noticed—at least, most of them didn't. Paul was an exception, being so reserved and dignified. He rarely raised his voice, even.

A super *mezé* was brought in, and fresh Greek bread baked in an outside oven. *Phetta* cheese and crisp water biscuits came too, and lastly a tray of sticky confections and a bowl of fresh fruit. Tina had a small pot of tea, and Paul drank Turkish coffee in a minute cup, along with a glass of iced water. *Bouzouki* music came over the air from the radio, and the scent of lemons was almost heady. They walked round the garden afterwards. Judas trees formed a small copse and it was close to this that the goats were grazing. Leda had said that they had decided to sell them and put the money towards the projected extension to the villa.

165

There was an evergreen thicket of shiny box, a shrubbery where oleanders grew in three shades of pink, and in scarlet and white as well. It was a pretty garden, and a pretty villa. The couple were lucky because Leda was an only daughter among five sons. They were all older than she, so they all had to contribute towards the provision of a dowry for their sister. It meant that the dowry had come more quickly than most, and that Leda and Costalis could marry while they were both still young. Leda had been explaining this while Paul was waiting for Costalis to make out the bill, and when Tina asked Paul later if brothers always had to contribute towards a sister's dowry she was told that this was the custom throughout Greece and Cyprus too.

'The boys in a family are not allowed to marry until all their sisters are married,' he went on. 'So you see, the female isn't too badly off after all.'

'You mean,' said Tina frowning, 'that even if a boy is in love he can't marry until his sister is married?'

'That's correct.'

'But supposing there are five or six girls and only one boy?'

'He helps his father to save for the dowries. He can't get married until the last of his sisters is married.'

'But that's ridiculous!' she exclaimed. 'It isn't fair at all!'

'It's custom, Tina. Some young men run off, to England or France or even to Australia, in order to escape the heavy liability of having to find dowries. A villa like the one we've been to can cost a small fortune these days.'

'Of course it can.' She paused in thought. 'What if there are, say, a dozen daughters and no boys?'

Paul gave a laugh.

'That would rarely happen—although I did hear of a farmer who had seven daughters and no sons. He was in such a small way that he gave up, resigning himself to having the girls on his hands until the day he died.'

'And did he?' enquired Tina curiously.

'Yes, he did.'

'No young men fell in love with any of the girls?'

'Oh, yes, I believe one or two did, but no young man will marry without a dowry.'

'The whole thing's crazy!'

'Everyone knows it is.'

'Then why, for heaven's sake, don't they abolish the idea?'

'It's an age-old custom, and age-old customs have a tenacious habit of sticking. No one

167

makes a start and so it goes on. The man feels he must have a dowry because when he becomes the father of a girl he will have to start at once saving for her dowry.'

'At once?' echoed Tina, diverted.

'As soon as a girl child is born her parents begin thinking of her dowry. Her aunts and cousins and grandmother—all the females in the family—begin embroidering bedspreads, table linen—oh, all sorts of things. These go into a chest smothered in camphor balls and come out only on the wedding day. Father begins saving for the rest of the dowry, which is usually a house but it can be money and animals.'

'What a stupid custom!'

'We shall probably be going to a wedding soon, so you will see what happens to all the beautiful things that are accumulated for the dowry—or for part of it.'

'We'll be going to a wedding?'

He nodded.

'Julia's cousin. She used to work for me, as housemaid. She's to be married at the end of next month and she is sure to invite me—and my new wife, of course.'

'It is customary for a servant to invite you to her wedding?'

'Don't look so surprised, my dear. Here in

Crete we do not have the same ideas about equality as you, or as other places in Greece, for that matter.'

She looked at him, recalling just how superior he could be at times, how arrogant and appearing to be full of his own importance. And now he was telling her that, in effect, he did not consider himself so much above one of his servants that he would refuse to attend her wedding. An enigma, a man whom she felt she would never understand.

They got into the car again and went home, to the beautiful villa which gave her a feeling of sheer joy each time she entered the high gates leading to the tree-lined drive. Two gardeners were busy in the borders; they eased up and lifted a hand in salute. Paul returned it as he swung the car to a halt outside the front door. Stavros opened the door, then went to put the car away in the garage.

'Thank you for a lovely afternoon, Paul.' She shone up at him, feeling happy because they had been together, and close.

'It was a pleasure, my dear.'

She went from him, up to their room, where she bathed, and changed into a long dress of shimmering lapis blue chiffon with a floating train and a detachable feather cape. Paul came in and she asked him to zip her up.

'I will, my child...but I'd much rather be unzipping you.' His voice was as soft as the tenderest summer breeze drifting in from a motionless sea. Tina lifted her face, twisting her neck, tempting him with her lips, aware of the intoxicating quality of the perfume she had just a moment ago sprayed on to her hair.

'Mind you don't catch my skin...' She quivered suddenly as his fingers slid into the back of her dress, moving slowly downwards, over her spine. His lips came down on hers, sensuously possessive, respect forgotten in the primitive desires that flared within his virile body.

'You little temptress,' he whispered hoarsely. 'My God, Tina, I never thought I'd feel like this about any woman!'

She pressed her body close so that he felt the gentle swell of her stomach, the wild uneven beating of her heart. She was tempting—with her body and her lips, with her eyes and the irresistible halo of her scented hair which she allowed to caress his face. He caught it in his hand; she cried out as her head was jerked back, waited breathlessly for the cruel mastery of the kiss that would reduce her to the level of a willing slave. She whispered, 'Take me, Paul, because I love you,' but it was to herself, silently. And yet she was not surprised that he

170

should know her thoughts.

The dress was eased away from her shoulders after the cape had been detached and fallen to the floor, seductive as a bridal veil. The dress followed; Paul urged her forward and she stepped away from the lovely garments. His arms embraced her; one hand sought again, this time within the lacy scrap of covering which matched the equally inadequate bra she wore. She felt dizzily swept to the heights of desire and when he swung her into his arms she let her head fall on to his shoulder in a little gesture of submission.

A long while later he was whispering, a hint of arrogance mingling with the amusement in his voice,

'Do you still maintain that I'm not your master?'

She lay still and silent within his arms, thrilling even now to the strength of his naked body melting into hers. Her husband said very softly,

'Answer me, Tina.'

She turned her face into his chest, rubbing her cheek against the wiry black hair. But he caught at her hair and jerked her face away from him, so that he could look into her eyes, eyes that were dark and drowsy with desire satisfied.

'Perhaps a little slap would help you to find an answer.' His voice was still soft, almost gently so, but within its accented depths there was a definite warning. Paul meant to have an admission from her that would satisfy his ego.

She said meekly,

'No, Paul, I d-don't still-still maintain that—that you're not my master...'

'And it makes you happy that I am your master?'

She had to admit that this was so.

'Yes, it makes me happy.'

He laughed quietly, the satisfied laugh of the conqueror. His was the superior position; she was his subservient wife. Typically Greek, she thought, and vaguely at the back of her mind was the conviction that she would be feeling angry later...but for now...she tugged his hand from her hair and snuggled down against him again, hoping that the dinner gong would not disturb them for a long while yet.

CHAPTER EIGHT

Dawn in all its glory streaked across the Grecian sky. Tina rose from the bed and slipped into a negligé, her tender glance going first to the man lying there, his dark head stark upon a snow-white pillow; his features in repose were almost like a child's, innocent, unmarked by time or the inevitable hurts of the world.

Impulsively she bent and touched his lips with hers. He stirred and murmured and lay still again. Tina smiled as she went over to the window. The curtains were parted a little; she drew them right back, using the silken cord with its tassel of intricately worked gold wire. A sigh of contentment issued from her lips. The dawn was wonderful! It was like the beginning of the world at the time when it trembled on the edge of birth, when from the mists of creation the purple bulk of the mountains emerged and took shape. The sea was oyster-pearl, the sky yellow and amber and jonquil gold. The great ball of the earth in its slow turning brought its edge to the sun, dipping as if

173

in homage to its superiority. The sun flared and it seemed that all the world was aflame. And then, even while she watched, all shapes and colours became sharp and pure, the gold alone spangled the lonely hills. Down in a tiny valley the tall campanile of a church shone white against the subtle greens and browns of the valley sides.

'Are you up?' The voice of her husband made her turn, a ready smile upon her lips.

'Yes; it's beautiful—It *was* beautiful, but you've missed it.'

'Missed what?' He sat up, rubbing his eyes.

'You look nice with your hair ruffled,' she said, her back to the window.

'Pass me a comb. Tidying one's hair is the first thing one should do on waking—for one's own self-respect and to keep the respect of others.'

Tina picked up a comb and took it to the bed. Paul caught her wrist and pulled her down so that she lay across him.

'You look like a little girl with your hair ruffled,' he teased, ruffling it a lot more.

'Are you working all day today?' she asked.

'Sorry, yes, I'm afraid so.' He combed his hair. Tina sat up and moved to her side of the bed, tucking her feet beneath her.

'Do you mind if I go into Heraklion? I want

to buy some shoes and a few other things.'

'Do I mind?' he repeated, frowning. 'What a question? Why should I mind?'

'I thought I'd ask, that's all.'

She went immediately after breakfast, driving the car herself. She parked it near Cornarou Square and walked leisurely to the shops. The city bristled with life, with traffic, people and noise. It was so different from the quietness surrounding her home and yet she was enjoying the change, being interested in all that was going on around her. Young girls in short dresses and spiky heels walked briskly past the older women who, dressed in black or other sombre colours, went far more slowly, their sun-bitten faces wrinkled, their eyes dull and half-closed, as if their owners were almost tired of living, of carrying on the struggle which their way of life imposed upon them.

'We in the West don't know how lucky we are,' Tina murmured as she strolled along, her eyes darting suddenly to another sight. A young girl in very modern dress was clinging possessively to the arm of a smartly-clad young man and, in incongruous contrast behind them, came a shepherd type man in *vraga* and heavy boots, his eyes fringed by matted black hair, his wife, dressed in dull grey homespuns, following a few respectful paces behind him, her

175

head sunk down so that her chin rested on the frayed collar of her jacket. Tina's heart went out to her. What had her life been through the long weary years? She'd probably brought numerous children into the world...a slave to the primitive passions of the man walking in front of her. Where were those children now? The sons might or might not be dead—killed as victims of the *vendetta*.

Depressed suddenly, Tina decided to go into an hotel and have some coffee. She had only just ordered when a voice at her side came softly to her, bringing a swift dark frown to her brow.

'So we meet again...' Dora's narrowed eyes glinted with something akin to venom. Her voice was silk-smooth, though, as she asked if she could sit down at Tina's table.

Tina nodded, thinking that it was ill luck that she had chosen this hotel in which to have her coffee, seeing that there were so many other hotels in Heraklion which she could have gone into.

'Of course.'

The girl took a seat, and clapped her hands to fetch a waiter. She ordered coffee and cakes, then leant back in her chair, her eyes fixed on Tina's face.

'Paul's not with you?' she asked softly.

'No, he has work to do.' Tina had no desire to be civil, even, and yet there was really no excuse for being otherwise.

'I'm puzzled about you and Paul,' Dora said without any attempt at tact. 'He and I had practically reached an arrangement. Then he went to England on business...' The soft voice trailed away to a bitter silence, and the venom returned to the dark, thickly-fringed eyes. The girl was beautiful, owned Tina, looking from the eyes to the clear wide forehead, the unblemished skin, the impressive, classical features, the long dark hair that shone like silk. 'He met you in England, and although I can understand his wanting you, since he has a reputation for seeking out certain women, what I cannot understand is his offering you marriage.' A pause, but of course Tina made no comment. The girl could continue if she wanted to, but at this particular moment Tina was determined not to be drawn into something which must assuredly end up in open hostility.

'He had a grudge against me,' continued Dora, speaking softly as if to herself. 'And he did say once that he would punish me one day...but marriage to an English girl, when he knows how his mother hates them...' Another pause, but still Tina remained silent. 'If he had asked you to be his pillow-friend I could more

177

readily have understood it.' Her eyes had moved from the contemplation of the vine-covered bamboo trellis in front of her and now she was looking at Tina—which was unfortunate for Tina because the girl's words had brought the colour into her cheeks.

Dora's eyes had widened, slowly; they were riveted on Tina's face and it did not need the perceptive quality in her voice to tell Tina that the girl had hit upon the truth. 'Pillow-friend...it would have been more like him to have insisted on your being that, and nothing more.'

It was the word 'insisted' that loosened Tina's tongue at last. Her colour deepened, but with anger this time.

'You appear to assume that Paul could have forced me to be his—er—pillow-friend, as you call it.'

'Don't act as if you've never heard the expression before,' snapped Dora. 'Your face just now gave you away. Paul did ask you to be his pillow-friend.' It was a statement, which Tina made no attempt to deny. Her mind was in conflict, because although she disliked the girl intensely, she was also sorry for her. She believed—though with extreme reluctance—that Paul had led Dora to assume he would marry her, perhaps not soon, but one day, when he had had a little more of his fling. Suddenly it mattered to Tina that he had this reputation. Before, it had seemed unimportant simply because she felt reasonably confident that her husband would never be unfaithful to her, that he would never have anyone else while he and she were together.

But now she was not so sure...

The doubts hurt, since she would rather feel she had full trust in her husband. Mingling with the doubts was a return of her fear of him, of the uncertainty as to how he would eventually turn out. She knew so little about him, about his inner nature, about the traits he had inherited from those pagan Bacchants of his tribe who still worshipped one of the ancient gods of Olympus, offering up sacrifices, dancing on hot coals in persuance of their orgiastic rites. His mother was one of them, closer by far than her son, who had been educated, who had in the course of this education absorbed some of the best of the Western culture. But as she had said to herself before, genetics were far more potent than environment. Paul was what his ancestors had made him, not a new product of the environment in which he now lived. Fear grew, even though she tried to shake it off. This girl sitting here had somehow awakened that fear, and Tina knew instinctively that she would not so easily shake it off this time as she had before.

Dora was speaking and Tina brought her mind back, listening intently as the girl said, 'You must have been clever to hold out against him, and in the end to have managed a proposal of marriage; he must have wanted you badly.' She paused, and it did seem that there was the hint of a tear in her eye. Again Tina's pity arose, and she bit back the angry retort which she was on the point of uttering. The girl went on slowly, 'He'll never be faithful, you need not fool yourself that he could ever be that. I was resigned, fully expecting him to have others, one after another, as he has always done. It's his nature—' She broke off, the bitterness in her eyes again, but the venom too. 'You should know what his nature's like. And you should know too that he's had numberless women before you. His finesse, the particular art he has of lovemaking, wasn't gained in the clumsy fumblings of youthful experiment. He's gained his art by practice—a great deal of practice.'

Tina's colour heightened as the girl spoke. She had wanted to halt the words, to make a wrathful protest but, to her amazement, she wanted to hear more. She was learning something about her husband. Not that she could learn anything about his lovemaking. It was as Dora had stated: he'd had plenty of practice...and that practice had made him the perfect lover...

The waiter came along with the coffee and cakes.

'Anything else?' He spoke in English; Dora answered him in Greek, shaking her head at the same time. The man departed and Dora spoke again.

'Have you met Paul's mother?'

'Yes, he took me to see her at her home in Patmos.' Tina poured herself some coffee and put milk into it, absently picking up the spoon to stir it even though she had forgotten to put the sugar in.

'She wanted him to marry me.'

Tina looked at her.

'You had the chance of marrying him, but you chose someone else. I don't believe that Paul would ever forgive a slight like that. He's too proud.'

'He has forgiven it. He was intending to marry me—before he went to England and met you!' The girl's nostrils flared; she dropped sugar into her cup so angrily that the liquid splashed up and stained the cloth. 'Aren't you troubled that he married you only because he couldn't have you as his pillow-friend?' she demanded after a pause.

'I am not willing to talk about my husband any more,' answered Tina coldly.

'You do realise that I have been his pillow-friend?'

Tina nodded.

'I gathered that,' she replied grimly, her thoughts flying to the way the girl had spoken about Paul's lovemaking. Again the hurt, agonising this time. It was crucifying to think of Paul making love to this girl, giving her all he was now giving his wife...carrying her on wings of ecstasy to the very heights of bliss. And yet why be hurt? It was an undeniable fact that he had had dozens before. But Tina realised that they could not hurt simply because she did not know them, nor would she ever know them. This girl sitting here was known to her; she could speak of intimacies with Paul, could own with a certain degree of pride that she had had Paul as her lover. Tina added, as the thought occurred to her, 'I have been told that Greek men never marry their pillow-friends.'

'Normally they don't, but with Paul and me it is different. We've been close for many years—before my marriage and since I was widowed.' Her accent became a little more pronounced as she spoke the last few words, but there was no emotion in her voice, not the mcrest hint that she had been upset on being widowed. Tina felt she was hard, and yet at the same time she knew without any doubts at all that the girl felt something for Paul, that her interest in him was by no means entirely mercenary. 'What did you think of his mother?' enquired Dora. 'I expect she treated you with some considerable hostility?'

'I just said I don't want to talk about my husband—and that includes his mother.'

'She has taken it very much to heart,' said Dora, ignoring Tina's protest. 'You have caused an estrangement between mother and son. She needs him; he's her only child.'

What was the girl trying to do? wondered Tina. What was her object? She must know, surely, that there was little closeness between Paul and his mother.

'She doesn't like me, but I don't think it affects her relationship with Paul.' Tina picked up her cup, sipped the coffee and then put it down again, reaching for the sugar.

'Paul will come to me in the end.' Softly-spoken words, but oh, what confidence was contained in them! Tina felt her fear become so real that it was a physical experience flooding her whole being. To lose him, to this girl...The fear of Paul himself seemed insignficant in comparison. 'He wanted you as his pillow-friend, and that in itself proves that he'll never be faithfull, for if you had agreed to be his pillow-friend he'd have tired of you eventually, you don't need me to tell you that.'

No, she did not, agreed Tina, but mentally. Paul had said the same thing, but in different words.

Tina drank her coffee and prepared to rise, glancing around for the waiter at the same time. Dora said, in that softly familiar voice,

'He married you only because he couldn't get you any other way.' It was a statement, but Tina found herself nodding automatically, as if she considered it to be a question. Dora went on triumphantly, 'It was just his way of getting what he wants—and so like him! He'll not hestitate to cast you off when he tires of the marriage arrangement.'

Tina looked at her; she had not risen from her chair and she leant back in it, watching Dora sipping her coffee, her dark eyes bright now as if the depression and the bitterness were erased. She had managed to prove to herself that Paul had married Tina only because he wanted her physically—which was true, of course. And now she was willing to play the waiting game, confident that Paul would one day come back to her.

Tina got up at last, her eyes smarting because

there were tears behind them, tears of fear and gradually dying hope.

Yes, she realised only at this moment that she had been cherishing the hope that her husband would fall in love with her. The revelation staggered her, since she had never consciously speculated on the possibility of Paul's being in love with her. It was too improbable a dream ever to come true. Even in her most optimistic moments the picture she drew was that of holding her husband by the physical attraction she undoubtedly had for him at this time, holding him for ever. She now saw that such optimism as that was just a pipe dream, indulged in to prevent her from brooding on what might one day come to pass: the request by Paul for a divorce. Divorce was easy, his mother had said. Tina knew this to be true, as her aunt had already told her how simple divorce was to obtain in Greece.

The waiter came over after she had beckoned; she paid him and, with a curt nod to the girl sitting there, she left the restaurant, wishing with all her heart that she had never entered it in the first place.

Paul wanted to know what she had bought. She showed him a blouse and skirt and some embroidered handkerchiefs. She was very quiet, her mind still filled with the conversation she had had with Paul's old flame. The girl had confidence and Tina admitted that it was not misplaced. One day Paul would go to her, ask her to be his wife. She would marry him, and give him those sons which his mother had spoken about.

It was much later that Paul said, an edge of puzzlement in his tone,

'What's wrong, Tina? You've been very quiet since returning from town.'

'Nothing.' But her voice was dull, and faintly hostile. 'Surely I can be quiet if I want to?'

He gave a slight start.

'You're touchy, aren't you? I only asked, because you don't seem too happy.'

'I'm happy enough,' she almost snapped.

She left him and went to their room, but after pacing about for ten minutes or so she went out into the garden and wandered away from the villa and the grounds, away into the peace and tranquillity offered by the silent loneliness of the hills. Only a donkey and a couple of goats for company, and a lizard that had stiffened on its sun-warmed block of stone. She sat down and it shot away; the air was pine-scented, the earth smelled freshly of rain, which had fallen in the night. Trees—carobs and olives and lemons with their shiny leaves—swayed slightly in the slow caress of the breeze drifting down from the pine-clad hills. The sky was an endless canopy of sapphire; the sun, lowering gradually towards the crest of the mountain, was pale yellow and gently warm—very different from when she had first come to Greece, in the hottest part of the year.

She moved at length, reluctant to return to the villa and yet forced to do so, simply because there was nowhere else to go. It was hurtful, feeling like this, with not an atom of enthusiasm for the presence of her husband. And suddenly she knew she had no desire for him any more. The idea of sleeping with him was—astoundingly—abhorrent to her. The revelation staggered her, sweeping over her with a tide of emotion that shook her to the very depths. For this was the situation in reverse! It was not Paul who had no desire for her, but she who had no desire for him!

She walked slowly, retracing her steps, trying almost frantically to convince herself that this feeling was, at worst, only temporary, but it was to no avail.

The bald truth was that she no longer wanted her husband as a lover...

It was inevitable that he should again mention her quiet, brooding attitude. At dinner she scarcely spoke, answering in monosyllables if he should ask a question. She was short with him or even hostile. She saw his eyes narrow on several occasions, his mouth compress, and a warning would force itself into her consciousness, telling her to beware. She ignored it. She could think only of what his mother had said, and of what Dora had said. Added to this was her fear of the man himself, the pagan she had married without even knowing what kind of man he really was. Oh, yes, she had known he had a reputation where women were concerned, and that his people were still among the few Greeks who held on to heathen worship, but, strangely, she had known no actual fear...not until recently, when she had begun to dwell, broodingly, because of words uttered by other people—his mother and his old flame.

She did not ask herself if she still loved him. She had always known that there would be only one man in her life whom she would love. Paul was that man, and she would love him till she died, but that did not mean that she was willing to make a complete slave of herself, a slave to his passions, to the primitive desires that were all that held her to him. She recalled with a sudden flush of humiliation her admission that he was her master...after he had coerced her, ordered her to admit it, his manner being threatening almost. She knew he would have made her admit it. Well, she had known she would be angry later and she was angry! Never again would he force words like that from her lips! Who did he think he was—a god!

She awoke to the sunshine as usual...but there was a difference this morning. Paul was not there, lying beside her in close intimacy. He was in the other room where, he said, he would spend the night, giving her the opportunity of getting over her 'tantrums' as he described her attitude when, after the studied silence of the dinner-table, she had said she was tired and that she would rather he found somewhere else to sleep. Staggered for a moment, he had stared in disbelief. But then his anger had flared; he had stated quite categorically that her bedroom was also his, and that was where he intended to sleep. A quarrel, tears and anger against white-hot fury and then icy contempt. Finally Paul had stalked from the room and into the adjoining one. The door had slammed and although Tina flung herself on the bed and wept as though her heart would break, it was with relief that she later stared at the closed door between the rooms.

Breakfast was a solitary meal, as Paul had already eaten and gone over to his study in the grounds. What to do now? Tina wondered. Life presented a dull prospect and she actually found herself forming a picture of total loneliness...with the divorce already going through.

They had lunch together but in silence; dinner was the same. Tina went to bed immediately afterwards and a long while later she heard her husband moving about in his room, and then silence.

This went on for almost a week, with scarcely a word spoken between them. But after dinner one evening Paul looked at her as she was about to go to her room. His face was grimly arrogant and she knew instinctively that the showdown had come.

'You needn't go,' he said in a rasping tone of voice. 'Sit down—there! I want to know what this is all about!'

She shook her head, scarcely knowing what to say. She was loath to mention his mother, and what she had said to her. She was still more loath to speak about the meeting with Dora. There was only one thing to do, she decided, and that was to invent some excuse for the change that had occurred in her attitude towards her husband.

She was pale as she faced him, declining the chair even though his gesture was imperative, as if it were an order in itself.

'I feel, Paul, that I shouldn't have married you, knowing you didn't love me. The circumstances were against me, against clear and logical thought. Had they been different I shouldn't have married you.'

Silence. He stared as if dazed from a blow that had come right out at him, from nowhere.

'Are you telling me,' he said at last in a dangerously quiet voice, 'that you now regret having married me?'

She nodded instantly, marvelling at the cool composure with which she was able to handle the situation.

'Yes, that is exactly what I'm telling you.' And although she felt she was lying to him, at the same time she knew for sure that, as things were, it would have been far better for herself if she had refused his offer of marriage in the same way she had refused the offer to be his pillow-friend.

The dark metallic eyes narrowed; the pagan features twisted into ugly lines.

'What has happened to bring about this change?' he demanded, holding his fury in check only by the greatest effort.

'I've been thinking that's all.' She shrugged lightly and would have turned from him, but her wrist was caught in a grip that made her utter a little squeal of pain and protest. Her heart began beating overrate and her pulses rioted in sympathy. The fear was there, potent and nerve-tightening. Nevertheless, she contrived a calmness which she hoped would deceive him, as she had no wish that he should become aware of her fear of him.

'Thinking, have you?' he snarled, his face close to hers. 'Well, you can begin thinking again! You might regret having married me but, by God, you *are* married to me and you'll keep that fact in mind!'

His face was white with fury; she wondered if he had forgotten that she loved him. But she had never said so, she recollected. She had merely assumed that he had made an intelligent guess owing to the way she was with him. Perhaps he had never made any such assumption; perhaps he had decided that she, like he, was merely being tender and loving because of the physical attraction.

'If by "keep that fact in mind" you mean that I must sleep with you, then it is you who can think again,' she told him quietly at last. For despite the misery that was filling her whole being, she still had no desire for him to make love to her. She had kept on thinking about Dora, who had been his old flame and then his light o' love, and who undoubtedly

192

would eventually become his wife. Yes, it was Dora who stood in the way, a barrier that could never disappear.

The grip on her wrist tightened, but although she winced and the tears started to her eyes, she made no sound, and within a moment he had released her.

'You're very arrogant, Tina,' he said, his voice more controlled, the ugly twist leaving his face. 'It's not you at all. There's something I don't understand, something you are keeping from me.' He looked down into her eyes and for a long moment there was silence in the room. She stared at him, her whole body quivering, her thoughts refusing to be drawn from the picture of Dora as his lover, and then as his wife. 'I shall make you tell me what is wrong. A girl like you doesn't change within a few hours.'

'It wasn't hours. I've been thinking, as I said, and I should never have consented to marry you knowing you had no love for me.' She still gazed up into his hard eyes, unaware of the unconscious pulsation of her heart that stemmed from the anguished desire that he would suddenly sweep away all her fears by telling her that although he had no love for her when he married her, he was now as much in love as ever a man could be.

'And what would you like to do about it?' he demanded with icy sarcasm. 'Ask me for a divorce...and a settlement?'

Her beautiful eyes blazed at the implication.

'I didn't marry you for your money, and you know it!'

'I don't know any such thing. In fact, I am beginning to convince myself that it was my money that tempted you, and nothing more.'

Tina shrugged, suddenly feeling very tired, and uncaring what he might think about her. She said, in retaliation,

'If it was, it's no more reprehensible than your reason for marrying me, is it?'

'Except that I was honest enough to tell you why I wanted to marry you.'

'And I expect you were intelligent enough to guess why I married you.'

The dark eyes glinted, points of steel shooting out from the burning embers of fury.

'So you're admitting that my money was the draw?'

'I haven't said so, but if you like to form your own ideas about it then what do I care?' So calm, and steady her voice, but—God, is he going to murder me! she thought, her mind inevitably conjuring up pictures of the Cretans with those evil-looking knives they carried...He was not a Cretan, she knew, but he definitely was an Anastenaride, which was probably worse.

He moved to touch her and she backed away, her mind numbed by the knowledge that his touch would be nauseating to her. The action infuriated him; she saw with a fascinated gaze the crimson threads of colour spiral up from the corners of his mouth to his cheeks, heard the low and guttural sound escaping like the deep-throated warning of a jungle beast about to attack its prey. Her legs were jelly; she expected them to collapse beneath her. Paul's face was a mask of fury as he came slowly towards her. With a sickening lurch her heart began to thud wildly against her ribs. Some access of strength came to her aid and she turned, swiftly reaching the door and wrenching it open. She was through it, flinging it to in his face. Terror gave her feet wings; she reached her room, went in and slammed the door behind her, turning the key. She listened, her heartbeats still thudding against her ribs. No sound. Perhaps he had gone out...perhaps he had gone to see Dora...

It was almost midnight when she heard him go into the other room, using the door opening out on to it from the corridor. He moved about the room; she heard the noise in the pipes that

195

told her he was showering. Tensed, she got out of bed, clad in a romantically dreamy djellaba, provocatively pleated and edged with handmade lace. It was fashioned by Gemma of Paris and had been bought by Paul in Athens. She had found it spread on the bed, put there by Julia when she made the bed, and although Tina had frowned at it, considering something plainer would be more appropriate to the situation in which she now found herself, she had put it on nevertheless, too lethargic to find something else.

Her nerves tensed suddenly as her husband's voice came to her from the other side of the door, which she had taken care to lock.

'I'm coming in, Tina.'

Fascinated, she watched the ornate, gold-plated handle go down. She guessed he was pushing at the door at the same time. A smothered oath, a louder,

'Open this damned door before I smash it in!'

Her lips went dry and she automatically licked them, spreading moisture that seemed instantly to dry up again. In her throat there was a choking sensation caused by fear that mounted and mounted until her whole body felt nerveless, ready to collapse. She tried to speak, but articulation was impossible; fear was an aching, agonising sensation now, robbing her of clear thought so that the idea of escaping by the other door never occurred to her, and she just stood there, numbed and resigned, watching the door jamb splinter as, after the third attempt, the powerful shoulder did its work and the door flew inwards.

Paul, white with fury, stood for a moment, getting his breath back. Then he came forward and at last she was given the strength to act. But it was too late. Tina reached the door and fumbled with the key. Paul, close behind her, reached for her wrist, twisting it with the merest flick of his hand but causing her such pain that a little moan issued from her lips.

'I'll teach you to lock the door on me!' he snarled. And he added, his face coming close to her own, 'If you are thinking of waking up the household I warn you to think again!— because I shall stop you, and in a way you will remember for a month!'

CHAPTER NINE

Tina began to struggle, finding strength that she believed had deserted her. Paul laughed at her attempts, his face evil above hers, his dark eyes pools of smouldering wrath.

'Struggle away,' he said. 'It'll afford me the greatest pleasure to prove to you, once again, that I'm your master!'

'Let me go!' she cried, intensifying her struggles. 'You have no right to—'

'I'm about to show you what rights I have!' he broke in, and before she knew it his head was lowered and his mouth, iron-hard and invincible, locked itself to hers in a kiss that was as primitive as it was possessive. He crushed her mouth, robbing her of breath, forcing her lips apart. His arms were like still hawsers, his body hard, demanding, arching to hers, felling the last of her resistance so that she lay limp against him, her soft young body bruised and aching. She would have fallen, when he released her, but his strong brown hands were firm beneath her elbows. The dark metallic eyes bored into her face before moving with pagan insolence to rove her curves, to regard with a half-sneer the lovely night attire she was wearing.

'I never thought, when I bought it, that I'd feel like ripping it off your back,' he said, and slid an arrogant hand into the slit at her thigh, bringing her to him with the same movement. The contact of his hand on her flesh was like an electric shock, and although she fought to quench the flame of her own desire she failed. His touch was the igniting force; he had no scruples as his hand probed further, the unbridled strength of his own desire inextinguishable. He hungered for her and she knew it.

She was swung right off her feet, carried across the room and with a jerk of his elbow the light was snapped off. Darkness flooded over her, and deep depression too. If only Paul had loved her...she would have surrendered so willingly. As it was, he took her by force, because she struggled inwardly, fighting her own primitive instincts, wanting only to be conquered in love, gently, tenderly and with respect.

It was not like that at all. There was no persuasion, no tender guidance through the path of yearning and desire to the realm of sweet surrender. And when his passions were spent, desire fulfilled, he had no gentle rein to lead her back with love and tender mastery, to rest within the haven of his arms. His was the use of dominance, of primitive unbridled mastery, to bring her to subjection, to crush the spirit that had had the temerity to rebel.

And then he left her, to lie awake and think, to make decisions and discard them, to lie in misery, feeling there was no hope for her, no light in her life.

The following morning she learned that the wedding they were to attend was fixed for a fortnight hence.

'I don't particularly want to go,' she said when Paul, after an early breakfast, came into the dining room while she was having hers. She felt her colour rise, turned her face away from him, aware as she was of his expression of mocking triumph.

'You will go, nevertheless.' So soft the tone, but inflexible. 'I shall be going to Athens on Friday until Tuesday. You can come along and get yourself a new dress for the occasion.' He paused and she said,

'I have no wish to go to Athens with you, Paul.'

'You will come with me because it's *my* wish,' was his quiet response. Another pause, but this time she made no comment. 'I believe I told you that I meant to entertain a little more now that I'm married. I shall be giving a dinner-party for some business associates while we're in Athens. I shall expect you to act as a newly-wedded bride should.'

She turned then, and shot him a glance.

'You're not asking me to act as if I'm in love, I hope!'

'You have the idea,' calmly and imperatively, 'see that you carry it out.'

'It's impossible!'

He came and stood over her, a tall and frightening spectacle in his black sweater rolled right up to his Arab-brown throat and with those iron-hard eyes piercingly narrowed.

'I advise you, Tina, to resign yourself to obedience. You're married to a Greek, remember, not to one of your spineless countrymen who've been misguided enough to make you their equals.' He saw the flash of defiance in her eyes and after a silent moment he added, in a dangerously quiet voice, 'If you put a foot wrong, Tina, you'll smart for a week.' He brought her face up with arrogant domination, because she had turned from him again, averting her head at the same time. 'I mean what I say. It isn't a fallacy that the Greeks are permitted to chastise their wives without fear of prosecution.' He released her, his eyes glinting in a way that warned her he was not talking for the sake of it, but that he was in deadly earnest.

She went to their room after breakfast and wept unrestrainedly. Her life was in chaos, and she felt somehow that she herself could have avoided all this dissension between her husband and herself. But the terrible fear that had resulted from the conversations she had had with his mother and Dora seemed to have swamped every other emotion, leaving no room for an examination of her real feelings. The terror put into her by Paul last night was proof and more that her fears were not imagined. He was a fiend with a temper that could reach conflagration heights. She knew that from now on her fear of him would grow and grow, until in the end she would be driven to leaving him.

Perhaps, she thought, it would be better to go now, before he could inflict any more hurt upon her, either physically or mentally. He had violated her body last night; just now he had violated her mind by sheer dominance and coercion.

The flight to Athens was made in silence. Orestes, the man employed by Paul to look after the flat, had heard from Paul and everything was ready for the arrival of him and his wife. Tina had already met him, and disliked him intensely. He had the smirk which she hated; he would look her over as if searching for some sign that she was expecting a baby. His very attitude, all the time, convinced her that, like most Greeks, his mind was almost always on sex. He would look at her legs, her hips, her breasts. The smirk often became a leer. She wanted to slap his sun-bronzed face every time she set eyes on him. What angered her more than anything was that Paul never seemed to notice. She felt that if he had noticed he would have given the man the sack.

'I have to go out immediately,' Paul said curtly ten minutes after their arrival at the flat. 'I shall be back in plenty of time for dinner. We'll go out for it.'

'Your friends are coming on Monday evening, you said?'

He nodded briefly.

'They're not friends exactly. More business associates.'

'How many are coming?' They were in the bedroom, with the curtains drawn back so that the golden view of the Acropolis in the sunbeams was visible, its temples etched in sharp relief against a sky of sapphire blue tinted here and there with pearl and white and a smattering of mauve. Tina's eyes moved, to the street below, where men hurried by, some twirling worry beads, some in pairs, their arms about one another. She turned back into the room, to face the tall dark Greek who was her husband.

'Four. Davos and Lefki Flourou, and Elias and Pelayia Mariakis.'

'Are they young?'

'In their thirties—Davos might be a little older—forty, perhaps.'

'Does Orestes do everyting?'

'Of course. He's very capable.'

She hesitated and then,

'Do you like him?' she asked.

'Like him?' frowned Paul. 'I don't think I understand?'

'I don't like him, that's all.'

A half-sneer caught his mouth.

'Are there any Greeks you like?' he enquired sarcastically.

She coloured.

'I don't think I've shown particular dislike of the Greeks,' she said defensively.

'You don't like my mother, or me, or Orestes—'

'Your mother doesn't like me,' she broke in tautly. 'I went to Patmos willing to be friends, even though you had warned me she doesn't like the English.' Her lovely eyes sparkled as they lifted to his. 'She wanted you to marry a Greek girl; it's a bitter disppointment to her that you've married me.'

He looked at her sharply.

'Has Mother said anything to you?' he demanded, his gaze fixed, in a searching scrutiny.

She managed to say without the hesitation which would have given her away,

'It was you yourself who said she was disappointed.'

He nodded then as if satisfied by her answer.

'I must be off. Are you all right for money?'

'Yes, thank you.'

'I'll give you some tomorrow, to buy the dress.' He paused a moment. 'You have something special for the dinner-party?'

'Yes, of course. I brought several evening gowns with me.'

He left her, alone with Orestes. Tina decided to go out right away, and not to return until she knew her husband would be in.

'You go out, Mrs Paul?' The smirk progressed to a grin that revealed several gold fillings. Every Greek male she had seen had gold fillings. Her aunt had told her that this was their way of collecting gold which could be used at some future date, if it should become necessary. The women also collected gold, but in the form of bangles, and it was not anything unusual to see a woman with down-at-heel shoes and shabby clothes wearing several lovely gold bangles on her wrists.

Almost the first person she met when she went on to the Acropolis was Bill. She looked at him blankly and said without thinking,

'Haven't you gone home?'

He laughed, as well he might.

'I got a job while I was here,' he explained. 'A great piece of luck. So I went back, gathered a few things—after working a week's notice, that was—and hopped on another plane. I've been here ever since.' He stopped and his eyes travelled with admiration over her figure, taking in the charming suit of fine woollen material. It was in a shade between coral and peach, and trimmed with beige embroidery on the lapels of the coat and round the hem of the flared skirt. Her bag and gloves matched; her shoes were of beige leather, flat-heeled for walking in comfort.

'Where do you work?' asked Tina interestedly. She was naturally remembering her husband's anger when she had spent the day with Bill, and her excuse the following day for not spending it with him again. He had taken it very well, since she had not given him any real explanation at all, being unwilling to tell him

206

the truth and equally unwilling to lie. So she had merely said she was sorry, but she could not keep to the arrangements as she had other things to do.

'I'm with the bank—' He mentioned it, going on to say that he saw the advertisement in the paper and went off and presented himself to the bank manager.

'It was in *The Times*, which as you know you can buy here,' he continued. 'They wanted someone who could speak English and French. I thought I'd lose the job because I'd no Greek, but they asked me if I was willing to learn and when I said yes they took me on. I had to give them references, of course,' he added finally.

'Greek's a very difficult language to learn,' she said in doubtful tones.

'I did classical Greek at grammar school,' he said.

'Oh well, that's a good start, isn't it?' They were in front of the Erectheum, the only people on this part of the site, although there were several coming slowly in this direction. 'Modern Greek's very different, though.'

Bill nodded in agreement.

'It's worth the trouble of learning,' he said enthusiastically. A pause and then, 'You're on your own again? Your husband attending to business, as before?'

'Yes. I shall see him tonight. You're not working today?'

'The banks are closed,' he said, indicating the time.

'Of course.'

'Will you join me for a drink?' he asked.

Tina hesitated, but only momentarily. She was not going to let her fear of Paul grip her to the extent of always having to avoid the company of other men. It was nice to be with an Englishman; she would enjoy a short break in a café, chatting with him. She smiled and said yes, she would love to join him for some refreshments.

They went to Constitution Square and sat at one of the tables under the trees. It was cool but not cold, as there was no breeze and the sun was still shining from a clear blue sky. Bill ordered a pot of tea and some sandwiches. He seemed happy at seeing her and this made her ask if he had made many friends yet.

'A couple, Greeks. They work at the bank and are both married. They were lucky, it seems, because they were telling me that if their parents hadn't been modern in their outlook they'd have never been able to marry for years yet.'

'They'd have had to work like slaves to give their sisters dowries,' submitted Tina, unable to keep the note of indignation from her voice.

'Have you ever heard anything so crazy as this dowry system they have here?'

'It isn't only here, Tina. I don't suppose *you* had to have a dowry,' he added with a laugh.

'My husband isn't like that anyway. Even if he'd married a Greek girl he wouldn't have wanted a dowry.'

'Some Greeks are dead set against it, but custom dies hard.'

'Yes, that's what my husband says.'

Bill said nothing. In any case, the waiter was coming with the tea and sandwiches. Bill paid him and he went away, saying thank you in English for the tip.

'Have you not got a girl-friend in England?' Tina did not know why she asked the question. She supposed it was just for something to say.

'Not anyone serious.' He stopped to look into her face. 'I expect you'll consider me impertinent, but I shall ask the question all the same. What made you marry a Greek?'

Tina coloured delicately.

'There's only one reason for marriage.' She felt rather pleased with her parrying cleverness in handling the situation.

'Mostly there is,' he agreed. 'But sometimes there are other reasons.'

She did not ask him what he meant. It was

far better to change the subject, which she did, asking him if he was going to travel while he was living in Greece.

'There are so many lovely islands,' she added. 'I believe there are over a hundred and thirty inhabited and almost two thousand altogether.'

Bill chose another sandwich and nodded his head.

'I shall certainly travel. I'd like to visit Santorini, and Crete again—oh, there are so many places. I guess I'd not have the chance to see them all even if I were to stay here a lifetime.'

She paused, her eyes on the sponge seller making his way towards their table. It was late in the season for a sponge seller to be about, she mused.

'I live on the island of Crete,' she said presently.

'Yes, you mentioned it before.' Bill hesitated a moment. 'You have this flat in Athens as well. Do you live in it very much?'

'No, not very much. The villa in Crete is much nicer.'

'Quieter, of course.'

She nodded. She sponge seller was at the table. She felt sorry for him and opened her handbag.

'Do you really want a sponge?' asked Bill, laughing.

'Not really, but I shall have to buy one. It's a purely selfish gesture as if I don't my conscience will trouble me.' There was laughter in her low, sweetly-modulated voice as she produced the money. 'Thank you, *efaristo poli!*'

'*Efaristo!*' The man looked pleased at making a sale and went optimistically to another table where a couple were sitting.

'He might have put it in a bag,' said Bill. 'Here, I've a plastic one in my pocket. Was intending to do some shopping, but it'll do tomorrow, anyway. I'd much rather spend my time here with you.'

Tina threw him a glance across the table. There was no mistaking the admiration in his voice, and in his large frank eyes. She wondered why she should be deriving pleasure from his company when she was in love with her husband.

'Yes,' she said, accepting the bag he was offering, 'it is pleasant, isn't it?'

He said quietly, watching her put the sponge into the bag.

'How long are you in Athens this time?'

'Until Tuesday.'

'I expect your husband will be attending to his business every day?'

She nodded, feeling guilty and not caring. Paul was not going to domineer over her, forbidding her to do this or that!

'Yes, he's usually fully occupied during the daytime.'

'I don't work tomorrow, not all day. Will your husband be working?'

'Most probably.'

A silence ensued, but she knew very well what would come at the end of it.

'Can we meet—and spend the day together?'

She did not hesitate because already she knew what her answer would be.'

'Yes, I think so. Have you a phone number, so that I can ring you if I can't come?'

Bill shook his head.

'I'm in an apartment in a small hotel in Kotzia Square,' he said, 'and they don't allow the lodgers to use the phone.'

'Not even to receive messages?'

'No. She's a funny old stick. Speaks hardly a word of English and neither does her son.'

'And yet they have an hotel?'

'They're mostly Greeks who use it. Tourists wouldn't even look at it.'

'Can't you get anywhere else?'

'Later. I'm looking around. I'm not at all happy. It's a funny old area with cheap shops and flea-ridden cinemas. A lot of loafers seem

212

to gather in the smaller square close by. It's not a pleasant district at all, and yet there's something fascinating about it for all its drawbacks.'

Tina fell to wondering what her husband would have to say if he knew she was spending her time with someone who lived in a place like that. Not that he would know, because if she was to be with Bill tomorrow she would make sure they weren't in Athens.

Another peddler approached and offered postcards and pistachio nuts, and again Tina paid out money for something she did not want. Bill seemed amused again, but this time he did not laugh. Instead, he regarded her with an odd expression as she accepted half a dozen postcards from the smiling dark-haired Greek.

'You're nice,' he said, unexpectedly, and she smiled faintly at the compliment. She looked at her watch, saw there was still an hour or more before she wanted to get back to the flat, and when Bill suggested they have a stroll around the shops she agreed, praying that Paul would not happen to see her with Bill. He had mentioned the part of the city he was going to and she knew it was a good distance from the area in which she and Bill proposed to walk.

But to her horror she saw Dora, coming along the street towards her; she turned swiftly, to become absorbed in some shoes in a shop window—men's shoes. Bill turned with her and Tina waited, her heart thudding, for the girl either to pass or to speak. Let her pass; let her not have seen me, she was saying to herself, but alas for her hopes. The voice was soft and silky, invidiously curious as Dora said,

'Tina—hello! Imagine seeing you here at this time! Where's Paul? Aren't you going to introduce me to your friend?'

Tina turned, contriving to keep cool as she made the introductions. Dora purred, determined to stay a few moments, chatting. Tina sensed that her object was to make her feel uncomfortable. Bill suddenly excused himself, having spotted one of his friends just a few yards away, along the street.

'There's something I forgot to ask him when we were at work today,' he said. 'I won't be a minute.'

He was away too long for Tina's peace of mind. Dora said silkily,

'Does Paul know you've a boy-friend,—an English boy-friend?'

'Bill is not my boy-friend,' snapped Tina, her heart still beating overrate, as she was convinced that Dora would, somehow convey the information to Paul that his wife was walking in Athens with Bill.

'You seem very friendly,' observed Dora, her dark eyes faintly mocking. 'Of course, it's only understandable that you'd be happy with one of your own countrymen. Where did you meet him?'

Tina's eyes blazed.

'That,' she quivered, 'is none of your business!'

Dora's brows arched in a gesture of pained surprise.

'There's no need to be so cross about it,' she chided. 'I only asked a civil question.'

'Please don't ask any more civil questions, because I have no intention of answering them!' Tina looked at Bill, and wished with all her heart that he had not left her alone with this girl.

There was a total dropping of pretence in Dora's next words.

'I wonder what Paul will say when he knows that you're spending your time with another man?'

Pale, and trembling inside, Tina said in a hollow voice,

'You're intending to tell him?' No sooner had the question left her lips than Tina realised her mistake. She ought to convince the girl that Paul would not be annoyed that his wife had found herself a companion for a few hours.

215

'If I should happen to see him I might mention it,' Dora said purringly. 'I myself found him to be fired with jealousy at the least sign that I was interested in another man.'

Tina decided to let that pass, though if she had been so inclined she could have retaliated by mentioning the man whom Dora had married. Paul must have been mad with jealousy at that time, thought Tina.

To her relief Bill came back. Dora seemed to sneer triumphantly as, staring directly into Tina's eyes, she murmured through her teeth,

'Goodbye. Enjoy yourselves. Give my regards to Paul, won't you?'

'Who is she?' asked Bill politely when Dora had gone.

Tina swallowed bitterly regretting having agreed to spend the afternoon with Bill. And yet anger mingled with her fear, since it was all wrong that she should not be able to please herself whom she spent these few hours with. She was doing nothing wrong...but her husband would not see it that way. Of this she had no doubts at all.

'She's a friend of my husband,' she managed to say casually at last.

'A beauty,' was Bill's only comment.

Half an hour later they were going their

separate ways, having arranged to meet tomorrow morning at half-past ten. They would take the trip to the island of Salamis.

Orestes was there but Paul had not yet arrived. Before Tina could get to the bedroom he spoke, his fillings gleaming as his lips parted in that smirk which Tina hated so much.

'Kyria Dora come one half hour ago,' he said. 'She say to see Mr Paul, but he not back yet. Kyria Dora say she see you with Anglais man—very friendly, no?'

Tina'a temper rose, filling her whole being.

'It is no business of yours,' she told him frigidly.

'No, Mrs Paul...' The smirk progressed to a leer. 'He very hots?—yes? Greek mans very hots—' The rest was lost as Tina, quite unable to control her action, slapped him across the face. He stared disbelievingly, the colour swiftly rising in his cheeks—not from the slap she had given him, but the result of anger. He looked ready to do her an injury. Here was another of the pagan tribe, she thought, not requiring much imagination to picture what would happen to the man's wife if she had given him that slap.

'Get out of my way!' she flashed. 'And in future know your place—and keep it!'

Once in her room she sat down on the bed,

every nerve quivering. It was not her nature to speak to a servant like that. At the villa she was well liked owing to the way she treated all those who served her. But with Orestes she had never felt comfortable, had never wanted to treat him as an equal. He was small and stocky, and far too deep for her liking. She often wondered why her husband had engaged him in the first place. He was a good and conscientious worker, so perhaps that was the reason.

To Tina's relief it was some time before her husband arrived at the flat, and the vivid red mark that she was sure she had made on the servant's face was no longer there. But something in the man's manner caused Tina's spine to prickle, caused her to suspect that he might say something to let Paul know that she had been with another man. However, he had obviously said nothing by the time they were ready to go out, and Tina decided that she had been mistaken. There was Dora, though. She would assuredly find some way of meeting Paul and telling him about Bill. For an undecided moment Tina did think of telling him herself, but she feared his wrath too much. After all, Dora might not meet Paul; he might never know that she had been with Bill.

'You didn't buy the dress then,' Paul was saying as they sat opposite one another in the restaurant to which he had taken her.

'No, I'll get it on Monday.'

'That's leaving it rather late. Get it tomorrow.'

'I shall have plenty of time on Monday.'

He shrugged his shoulders.

'What have you been doing today?' he asked, changing the subject.

'Oh, nothing much. I went on to the Acropolis.'

'The place seems to draw you. You go up there every time we come to Athens.'

'It draws me,' she admitted. 'I could go up every day of my life. You find peace no matter if there are crowds. You feel the presence of ghosts from the past—' She broke off, unwilling to enter into a conversation with Paul. She just wanted to be quiet, and think.

The first two courses had been served when, glancing at her husband, she saw his expression change. She turned her head, and the wine in her glass spilled on to the cloth when she saw who it was who had caught Paul's attention.

Dora! How did she come to be here, at the restaurant where she and Paul were dining? This was no mere coincidence! She suddenly remembered Paul saying over his shoulder, as they were leaving the flat,

219

'We'll be at the Dawn Palace, if for any reason I should be wanted.'

Had Orestes told Dora where they would be? Tina could not make any sense of it, but she was certain that if she could have a starting point from which to work it out, she definitely would be able to make sense of it.

'Dora.' Paul rose as he spoke, his dark eyes flickering to his wife, obviously to see how she would take the intrusion. She maintained an impassive countenance; Paul's mouth compressed and she realised at once that he intended to have the girl sit down with them...just to get even with his wife. 'You're alone? You must join us—' He beckoned a waiter and asked that another cover be laid. Meanwhile, he handed Dora into his own chair and sat in the one brought immediately to the table. Tina, pale even to the lips, waited with a sort of expectant resignation for what would happen. She was not wrong in thinking that Paul would give some attention to his old flame. Tina had treated him with cold reserve and he meant to pay her out. His manner towards the girl awakened jealousy so strong that the barbs inflicted an almost physical hurt. But she contrived to assume an indifferent air, determined to convince him that she did not care.

The two chatted, leaving her out of the

conversation; it was plain that Dora was puzzled, which was understandable since she was not
to know that an estrangement had occurred
between Paul and his wife.

When at last the girl did speak to Tina it was
to say, in that silky voice, but with a distinct
undertone of triumph,

'Did you tell Paul we'd met in Athens this
afternoon, Tina?'

The look which Tina gave her was glacial.

'No, I didn't feel it was important to him,'
she said.

'You met in Athens?' Paul looked at his wife.
'Why did you feel it was not important enough
to mention?'

She shrugged carelessly, her eyes on Dora's
lovely face. Did the girl mean to play a cat and
mouse game with her? she wondered.

'We didn't have much time for conversation
before we came out,' she reminded him. 'You
were late returning to the flat.'

'Tina was with a charming young man...
weren't you?' she purred. She had begun with
the third course, saying firmly that she was
not very hungry and therefore she was not
at all troubled at missing the first and second
courses. She concentrated on her food after
saying the words she had obviously come
here to say. It was to be no cat and mouse

game, then. Dora had obviously been impatient to see what the result of her pronouncement would be. Paul's piercing regard was fixed on his wife's face, but to her amazement he smiled immediately Dora glanced up, smiled and said interestedly,

'A young man, my dear? Was it anyone I know?'

Tina's surprise was soon dissolved in perception. Her husband was not intending to give Dora any satisfaction from what was only too starkly a case of deliberate tale-carrying. Well, thought his wife, that was certainly something to his credit. Falling in with his mood, she answered lightly.

'No, Paul; it was a young Englishman I'd met previously.' She paused...and trembled inwardly because of the look in his eyes that warned of punishments, later, when he had her alone...and at his mercy. She swallowed convulsively, but the lump born of fear remained stuck in her throat and it was with difficulty that she managed to keep her voice clear and steady as she continued, 'He was on holiday at the time, but he found himself a job in the bank and he now lives here.' Tina's glance flickered to Dora. Her face was a study; it was plain that she was put out by the failure of her malicious intent to cause trouble between Paul

222

and his wife.

'Ah the young man, Bill—I think you said his name was?' Again that smile from Paul, and the interested expression had returned to his eyes. No one, reflected Tina, would believe that under that veneer he was seething with fury, planning what he would do to his wife once he had her back at the flat. 'So he's working in Athens? That'll be nice for him. Perhaps we should invite him to dine with us one evening?'

Tina's eyes widened, meeting his and conveying several things all at once. She thanked him for sparing her humiliation before his old flame; she let him know that she understood his own feelings, and she conveyed to him the fact that she was terribly afraid of him. His eyes were impassive, as if he were totally unaffected by the revelations in her wide and almost pleading gaze.

She said through whitened lips,

'Yes, Paul, it would be a very nice gesture if we invited him to dinner. He hasn't made many friends yet—just two, who work with him at the bank.'

Dora was sitting quietly eating her food. There was a frown on her brow and each time she stopped eating her mouth went tight. Tina saw Paul look at her...and it certainly did seem that the only expression in his stare was one of contempt!

Contrary to his usual custom of taking Tina for a last drink in the lounge, after they had had their dinner, he said he was rather tired and wished to go home at once. He called a taxi for Dora, who was staying as usual with her friends at Gylphada, and then he and Tina were on their way, also in a taxi. She tried to speak several times but failed. Paul was so formidable, sitting there, his profile more grim-looking than she had ever seen it before. What was he intending doing to her? She supposed that if she'd any sense she would have refused to enter the taxi, would have said she was staying the night at the hotel. But the idea was soon accepted as absurd, as she had no clothes with her, and in any case, Paul would hardly have allowed her to approach the desk with a request like that!

He spoke at length, when they were almost at their destination.

'What are you thinking, Tina?'

She was silent for a space and then, in a hollow little voice that should by rights have melted even the hardest heart,

'I'm—I'm afraid of—of y-you, Paul...'

He made no answer, nor did he turn

his head. She wondered if he had heard. Perhaps not, she thought, since she was sure her words had been less even than a whisper.

CHAPTER TEN

Despite her fear of him Tina was able to face him bravely when, a quarter of an hour later, she was alone with him in their room at the flat. Immediately they arrived there he had ordered Orestes to go and stay with his sister, who lived close by. The servant's shifty eyes had moved from Paul's face to Tina's, and then his thick eyelashes had come down, hiding his expression. Knowledge hovered on the brink of Tina's brain and she felt that if only she had a few minutes on her own she would solve the mystery of how Dora had come to be at the Dawn Palace, and also that of Orestes' previous attitude towards Tina, which was not only far too familiar but had bordered on a threat.

'So you flaunted my authority and met this Bill again?' Paul was standing close, towering above Tina who, having discarded her cloak, was staring up at him, her slender figure quivering beneath the floral-printed fine lawn evening gown she wore. 'You did understand, I take it, that my reaction to the information was merely a pose?'

She nodded, passing a tongue over her parched lips.

'Yes—and I th-thank you for sparing me—me humiliation in front of that—that creature!' The word shot out in an explosion of rising anger. 'She didn't have the satisfaction she expected.'

Her husband's dark eyes glinted. He was not interested in Dora, but only in his wife's disobedience. She sensed the white-hot fury that was taking possession of him.

'Did this fellow know you were here in Athens?' he demanded. 'Have you been corresponding with him?' His voice was soft but vibrantly menacing, and Tina automatically stepped back in a little access of self-protection. She put a quivering hand to her heart, because its mad throbbing frightened her. What a position to be in—alone with a man who could put sheer terror into her like this! How had she come to marry him in the first place?

'No—no, Paul—he and I haven't been corresponding. We m-met by accident this afternoon and—'

'Don't lie!' The fury within him could no longer be restrained; he strode across the room, grasping her arm and twisting her body so that it came hard against him only to be thrust off

227

again as Paul shook her with such violence that her teeth rattled and it seemed for one dizzily unconscious moment that the very breath had left her body. 'I ought to treat you like a Greek wife and take a whip to your hide—' He shook her again, untouched by the cries she made, the little pleading moans, the tears that flowed unrestrainedly down her ashen cheeks. 'You regret your marriage to me, you said, but by God, you'll not be allowed to *forget* your marriage—nor will you flaunt your husband's authority. Do you know what you'd get if you were married to a Cretan?'

She shuddered and burst into tears again.

'Leave me alone,' she sobbed.

'You'd be whipped until you were ill! And this Englishman would be slain—knifed! That's what would have happened had you been married to a Cretan!'

He still held her, his fingers pressing mercilessly into her tender flesh. She said through the sobs that racked her body,

'Let me go! You've punished me enough—'

'Are you seeing this man again!' he demanded through his teeth.

Tina started to shake her head, then stopped. Something beyond her control surged up, swamping her terror as if by magic. She lifted her head, a sparkle of defiance entering her eyes.

'Yes, I am! So there! We're spending the day together tomorrow—going to Salamis! I'm not being dictated to by you—a—a *foreigner!* A pagan without a notion of how a woman should be treated! I shall see him whenever I want, now that he's living in Greece, and there's nothing you can do about it! Nothing!'

A terrible silence followed her words. She stared up into the face of a fiend. And the spurt of courage melted as fear took over again.

'So there's nothing I can do about it...' Never had Tina heard such a threatening intonation in his voice! She had several times asked herself if there was murder in his heart, but now she was wondering if it were torture he was intending to inflict upon her. She jerked her body, an action born of terror mounting almost to paralysis. She felt that if she did not move now she would never move again, not as long as she lived. But the action of racing to the door galvanised her husband into action too and she was caught within seconds, caught in an embrace so savage and uncontrolled that she felt her senses leaving her. Tears flooded her eyes and rolled unchecked down her face. She struggled desperately, pummelling his chest with her fists, jerking her body in an attempt to free it from his hold. The hem of her dress somehow got under his feet; another jerk of her body tautened the dress, causing the snap fasteners holding the shoulder straps to give way under the pressure. The lovely garment fell to the floor, leaving Tina in the scantiest of underwear.

Paul stared, first at the dress, lying there at his feet, and then at Tina's near naked body. Her heart sank as she saw his expression. She made no further attempts to struggle when, inflamed by the primitive passions she had experienced so many times before, he caught her to him, savagely, possessively, smothering her little cry with the pressure of his mouth on hers. His lips were pressed against her teeth, trying to force them apart and in the end they succeeded. His hands strayed, showing her their mastery...and their rights. She shivered, unable to feel anything but revulsion. It was inevitable that he should sense this revulsion and the result was another demonstration of his fury. She was almost fainting when at last he lifted her, carrying her across the room to the bed. The slender brown hands removed the garments; his voice was low and throaty as lying down beside her after he himself had undressed, he said,

'You're mine—understand! If you so much

as look at this other man again I'll kill you!'

Paul did not go out the following morning and Tina, pale and feeling physically ill, could only think of Bill waiting there, wondering what had happened that she could not keep the appointment. At last she said to Paul,

'Do you mind if I go out?'

The dark eyes glittered dangerously.

'For what reason do you want to go out?'

'Bill'll be waiting—'

'Then let him wait!'

'It isn't fair.' She paused, waiting for him to say something. 'We did meet by accident, no matter what you think to the contrary.'

'But you weren't meeting by accident today.' He spoke quietly yet with a harsh inflection. But there was another quality in his voice, one that Tina might have interpreted if her mind had not been absorbed with Bill.

'Can I go and tell him I can't come?'

'No,' he said brusquely, 'you can't.'

She looked perceptively at him.

'You think I won't come back?'

He was silent for what seemed an eternity.

'Would you come back?' he asked curiously.

She was honest enough to say,

'I don't know, Paul. You and I are so

231

different. I said I was afraid of you and I meant it—' She broke off, shuddering at the memory of his brutality, and he frowned at the sudden appearance of moisture in her eyes. 'A wife should not—not have to endure such treatment.'

He looked at her straightly.

'Who caused all this, Tina?' he asked her softly.

Her lip trembled. For a moment she felt she must tell him everything—about his mother and Dora and even Orestes. And she would tell him of her fear too, and the reason why it was growing all the time. She would say that it was because he belonged to that pagan tribe, relic of the worshippers of the god Dionysus—god who represented all that was bad in man, all that was dark. Not like Apollo who stood for all that was good...Her thoughts drifted off the subject. She knew she could never tell him any of this. He would be angry with his mother; he would demand an explanation from Orestes. It was not worth causing all this trouble, she decided. But she did ask again if she could go and see Bill. Paul again refused and she let the matter drop. Bill would probably guess that her husband was not working after all.

'Tina, I asked you a question.'

She nodded as her husband's voice came to

her through the silence.

'I suppose it was my fault,' she admitted, surprising herself by the confession.

'You discovered that you don't want me any more—at least, that was what I had gathered.'

She said that this was true.

'Marriage is no use without love,' she added. And, when he made no comment, 'Ours is purely physical attraction, and that's not a strong enough foundation for a successful union. But apart from that, you and I are too different ever to make a success of marriage.'

'East and West don't mix, is that it?'

'Yes, that's exactly what I mean.'

'You and I were admirably suited at first,' he reminded her. 'You wanted me as much as I wanted you. Something occurred to bring about a change in you, but what it was I cannot even guess.' He looked at her and now there was nothing harsh or arrogant in his dark, thickly-fringed Greek eyes. 'Won't you tell me, Tina?'

She shook her head.

'You're imagining it,' she said, and he shrugged his shoulders and said tersely,

'If you say so, Tina.' And that was all. He later said they would be going home first thing in the morning. He had changed his mind about having a dinner-party.

'You're putting it off?' she said disbelievingly.

'Yes. I'll phone them later. If there had been
any chance of a plane today we'd go, but I
don't think there is. However,' he added as an
afterthought, 'I could phone the airport and
find out.'

Tina said perceptively,

'It's because you're afraid I'll run away, isn't
it?'

To her surprise he nodded without a second's
hesitation.

'I'm taking no chances. In the mood you're
in at present you are likely to do something
you'll regret.'

'Such as?'

'Enlisting the aid of this Englishman in getting back home.'

'I don't need anyone's help, Paul. If I did,
though, it would be my aunt and uncle I would
go to.'

He looked at her and his eyes were brooding.

'You like this man. I sense it, so it's more
than feasible that you would go to him.'

'I do like him...' She let her voice trail, aware
that Paul would misunderstand the reason for
it but not caring if he did. She was thinking
of her love for Paul, knowing that whatever he
had done to her, and whatever he would do in

the future, she would always love him.

And her love was not measurable by sex, and the attraction she had felt for him until recently. It was measurable by the spiritual feelings she had towards him. She loved him for himself...loved a pagan with whom she knew for sure she could not live. No, deep within her heart she had known that they must part. There was no future for them. He was too different from her in so many ways. Added to this was the fact that he did not love her.

He managed after all to book seats on a plane leaving late that afternoon. He never allowed Tina out of his sight although she assured him that although she felt she would leave him, she would not do so immediately.

'I shall never give you the chance of leaving me,' he told her harshly. 'I said last night that you are mine! You will stay mine—for ever!'

She allowed that to pass without comment. When the time came she would leave, no matter what he said at this present time. He would have to go to Athens on occasions; this would be the time she would choose to leave Crete, and Greece. He would divorce her eventually, and marry Dora, then his mother would be satisfied.

He seemed to be very restless all morning and several times Tina had glimpsed a look of

235

brooding dejection in his eyes. She said eventually,

'Let's go out for a walk, Paul.' She still felt physically ill from the experience of last night, but anything would be better than sitting here, looking at one another, saying nothing. Paul agreed and they went out, but as they reached the street she felt cold and decided to go back for a heavier coat. As there was no way she could escape other than the door by which they had emerged, Paul did not accompany her back into the flat. She was part way through the hall when she stopped at the sound of Orestes' voice. He was on the telephone, which was in a small apartment which Paul used as an office.

'Yes, there was trouble. My master was white with the fury, but he send me to my sister for the night and I think it because he could beat wife for going with this other man, because you say you tell him. You say you will give me five hundred drachmae for telling you where they are dining. If you will leave it with my friend, Kypros, at the...' His voice trailed and his jaw dropped as Tina, having walked silently into the office, came to a halt by the side of the desk. Before he could speak into the receiver again she knocked it out of his hand and then, picking it up, replaced it on its rest.

'And now,' she said determinedly, 'you can talk to *me!*'

He glared at her, then at the receiver.

'I talk for to order groceries—'

'You were talking to Kyria Dora,' she broke in softly. 'I want to know what it was all about!' Inside she was all shaken up, her nerves not having recovered from last night, but outwardly she appeared calm, and very much in control of the situation. 'Last night, you told her where my husband and I were dining—'

'I not tell her anything!'

'I have just heard you mentioning the five hundred drachmae she is paying you for the information.' To her satisfaction the man's face went grey, and his fists opened and closed convulsively. 'I will tell you now that I guessed there was some plot, or something peculiar, being hatched between you and Kyria Dora, simply because it wasn't possible for her to have come upon us by accident—even though my husband did not suspect anything. However, he didn't know that Kyria Dora had been here, did he? But I did, and I also knew she had told you she'd seen me with a gentleman friend. Why did she tell you that?' demanded Tina. 'Answer me! Why?'

The man shrugged his shoulders.

'I think I don't know.'

Her eyes glinted.

'Then think again, Orestes,' she recommended softly. 'I can get you the sack, remember. And I happen to know you have to help with a dowry—'

'Not get me the sack!' he almost shouted. 'It cruel fate if I gets the sack!'

'You should have thought of that sooner.'

'Five hundred drachmae was tempt—was of the tempt! I give to my father for the dowry!'

'Why did Kyria Dora tell you she saw me with a gentleman?'

The man hesitated, but eventually his body sagged and he answered,

'She believe I tell my master.'

'But you didn't tell your master.'

Another hesitation.

'If I tell you everything, you not tell Mr Paul? You not get me for the sack?'

She shook her head, but only after a long moment of considering.

'No, I shan't tell Mr Paul.'

'I think I like to make love to you—'

'*What!*'

'I like you with the fair hair, and think you hots, because my master hots—have many hots Greek girls that I know of! Many English girls like all the time—morning and afternoon and night, so I think if you are hots like that you like me to—'

'*Orestes!*' The thunderous voice of Paul broke in on the man's words like a shot from space. Tina spun round, every vestige of colour leaving her cheeks as she caught the murderous expression on her husband's face. 'What the hell are you talking about?'

Orestes' face was the dull grey colour of wood-ash; his whole body shook like a jelly.

'My master...I think you have gone for walk, and Mrs Paul not want to go, so come back—'

'What were you talking about?' thundered Paul, stepping forward as if he would strike the man across the face. 'Answer me before I put my fingers round your throat!'

Orestes cringed; Tina thought he was going to cry. But instead he began talking, in Greek.

'In English!' rasped Paul, 'and quick!'

Orestes began at the beginning and although it was plain to Tina that her husband had been within hearing distance long before his thunderous exclamation was uttered, he listened intently to every word his servant was saying.

'I didn't tell you that Mrs Paul with man because I think that if I—I—threaten her with me telling you, she then let me—me—' He got no further. Tina uttered a strangled little cry at the force of the blow which her husband delivered to the face of the man before him. Blood spurted from Orestes' upper lip, but the wound was superficial.

'Carry on!' ordered Paul, his own body trembling now, with the fury that enveloped him.

'Mrs Paul slap my face—'

'She slapped your face? You actually made advances to her?'

Tina intervened to explain what had happened.

'He didn't get as far as making advances, Paul,' she added.

Paul turned to his servant again, ordering him once more to continue with his story.

'Kyria Dora ask me to telephone her to tell her if I talk to my master about the young Englishman being with his wife. I say no and Kyria Dora angry and ask me where she find you. I say if she give me five hundred drachmae I tell her.' He stopped, and cowered away, fearing another blow from that steel-hard fist.

It was only to be expected that Paul would send the man off at a minute's notice, but he did surprisingly give him his wages, although only after Tina had pleaded with him to do so.

'I'm sorry it's all happened,' said Paul after the man had gone. 'You should have told me he treated you like that.'

'It doesn't matter now,' she said.

'I knew Dora was jealous of you, but I never for one moment thought she'd go to lengths like those.' He sounded utterly dejected, and Tina wondered if it were disappointment in the girl that was causing it. She heard him say, after a long while,

'I don't suppose this makes any difference to us?'

'Why should it?'

'No reason—none at all.'

The wedding of Julia's cousin was a typical village affair, many of the guests being invited as much as three days before.

When Tina and Paul arrived excitement was high. The bridegroom was being shaved by the priest, while the bride's maidens were decorating the bed, tying ribbons to the corners and laughing as they did it. The lovely linen and blankets and cushions were put upon it. It was rolled up and carried to the bride's dowry house where the bride, assisted by several of her young relatives, was being got ready for the ceremony. *Bouzouki* music blared forth from loudspeakers, raucous laughter followed the telling of some lewd joke by one of the several 'best men' in attendance on the groom. Piglets were being roasted on spits, and bread was

241

being baked in the huge outdoor ovens. The sun was shining, but the wedding feast was being held in the *cafenion* in the square, because the weather was not warm enough to have it in the open—in the orchard adjoining the bride's house, where it would have been laid out on long tables beneath the lemon trees if the wedding had taken place in the summer or early autumn.

In the church all seemed to be chaos, with guests continuously taking snapshots of the couple, the priest, and of each other.

'It's like bedlam!' exclaimed Tina, forgetting for the moment to be cool with her husband. 'Don't they have any respect for the church?'

He laughed, and she felt saddened all at once because it seemed such a long time since she had heard him laugh.

'Not much,' he admitted. 'Everyone seems to think they can talk at once.'

'You can't even hear the priest!'

'He doesn't seem to mind.'

'The couple look very happy.'

'A wedding is usually a happy occasion,' he said, and it did seem that there was an edge of bitterness to his deep, accented voice.

Everyone was leaving the church at last and the feasting began, but the couple did not take part. They danced, and the guests came forward in ones and twos to pin paper money on their clothes.

'They must have a fortune!' gasped Tina.

'It's usual for them to get hundreds and hundreds of pounds.'

'It'll go towards the first daughter's dowry, I suppose.'

'Probably.'

'Perhaps the system will have died out by that time.' She thought of the children she herself might have had, and again a sadness swept over her. Life with Paul was no longer one of fear, as he and she had occupied separate rooms since their return from Athens. Paul seemed to have a guilt complex and Tina could not make out if it was owing to his savage treatment of her or because of what Dora had done. It did not matter. What did matter was that she was unwilling to go on like this. She wanted more than Paul was willing to give. She wanted love. But although she was determined to leave her husband, she seemed to be drifting on, unable to form any definite plan. This was easy while their lives were following the present lines, but if he should again take her by force she would have no hesitation in leaving him immediately. She suspected that he knew this, and it could be part of the reason why he was leaving her alone.

243

'You're quiet.' His voice came to her and she turned her head. She was drinking *raki* and not liking it very much, but she had learned long ago that it was an insult to refuse what was offered at a feast. On the tables were stacks of food—the piglets, deliciously browned, roast lamb and chickens, succulent watermelon and other fruits, with warm bread, fresh green salads, and many more mouth-watering delicacies.

'I'm just enjoying it all,' she returned. 'Are you enjoying it, Paul?'

He nodded, but she noticed a frown as well. He would be glad when it was all over.

But it was very late before the guests began to depart, and on reaching the place where he had parked his car Paul found himself completely hemmed in.

'It looks as if we're to be here even longer than I expected,' he said, his tone good-humoured enough but sounding tired, dejected. The familiar arrogance had not been in evidence for some time, and always when he spoke to Tina now it was as an equal, never dictatorial as it had been before that visit to Athens.

'Some of the cars are moving now,' she said. The moon was up, but the clouds kept obscuring it and all the people were switching on their headlights. It was totally without order, and the noise was deafening—people laughing and calling to one another. Cars revving up; horns blaring quite unnecessarily, children racing about all over the place.

About a quarter of an hour passed and then Paul said he thought he might be able to manoeuvre the car out from between two which had parked very close.

'Some of those in front have gone, so I think I'll be able to manage it,' he added. But it was found that the passenger door would not open sufficiently for Tina to get in, and instead of doing as Paul said and slipping in via his door, she said she would wait, making her way to the place where she knew he would emerge from the spate of vehicles with which he was surrounded.

She dodged in and out, making for the space. A car door banged suddenly and the driver, seizing a chance to get out, revved up and set his car roaring forward before anyone else could baulk him. But Tina's coat had got caught in the door and even before she had time to cry out she was being dragged along with the car. A scream rent the air as a child saw what was happening. Tina's coat eventually came away from her body and she went hurtling backwards, right in front of her husband's moving

245

car. There was a screech of brakes, a medley of voices, people pressing round, getting in the way. But Paul broke through and swept her into his arms.

'Oh...my head!' she moaned, and let it fall on to his shoulder.

It was several hours later that she came to in the hospital at Heraklion. A uniformed nurse was there, and put a cool hand on Tina's brow. Memory flooded in and for some absurd reason she started to cry. A doctor came within seconds after the nurse left the ward. A middle-aged, thick-set Greek, he smiled down at her and said,

'No need for tears, Mrs Paul. You are a very fortunate young lady.'

'I—I'm not hurt, th-then!'

'A little, but if it hadn't been for your husband's presence of mind, and the incredible way he managed to avoid hitting you, you might have sustained an injury to your head that could have had the most dire results.' He was feeling her pulse, and then he was speaking again. 'You've given your husband a fright, I can tell you! He's in a far worse state than you are.'

'Worse state?' She frowned up at him from the pillow. 'I don't understand?'

'You will, when you see him. I'll send him in.'

Paul came immediately and as she looked into his face she scarcely recognised him. He seemed to have aged ten years or more; his face was drawn and haggard, his eyes glazed, his colour changed even, from a rich bronze to a dull sallow-tinged brown.

'Thank God you've come round—' His voice broke in the middle and she saw him swallow over and over again as if in an attempt to remove some painful blockage in his throat. 'The doctor kept assuring me there was nothing seriously wrong, but you didn't come round—' Again he stopped, and he closed his eyes for a few silent moments. 'Tina, my love, my little wife...I thought I'd lost you. When I saw what was happening I couldn't think, and yet I knew I had to act—' For the third time he broke off, shaking his head as if to clear it. Tina spoke, softly, wonderingly, as she fluttered him a smile,

'You love me?' He merely nodded and she smiled again and said, this time with a sort of quiet joy in her sweet young voice, 'You really love me—and I didn't know...' She paused a moment. 'I should have told you that I loved you...oh, but I wish I had!'

'You—love me?' Paul shook his head disbelievingly. 'Is it true?'

She was given no opportunity of answering, as the doctor returned and Paul was ordered to leave. She had to smile, because he went so meekly, which was not like him at all!

'There has to be a small operation,' she was told later. 'It's nothing to be alarmed about and you'll be over it and home within the week.'

And she was. Her husband came for her, looking much more like himself, the drawn expression gone from his face and his colour restored. He had visited her every day, staying for as long as he was allowed. All the misunderstandings had been cleared up, and Tina learned that her husband had very soon realised that he was falling in love with her and he almost told her so on several occasions, feeling almost sure that what she felt for him was love. But as he could not be absolutely sure he allowed his pride to hold sway over his emotions and so the words Tina longed to hear were never uttered. She explained that she felt he knew she was in love with him and all she wanted was for him to love her.

'But I never really had any hope,' she confessed, and she went on to tell him that she felt sure he would divorce her and marry Dora.

'Divorce?' For a few seconds she saw all the

old familiar arrogance, the mastery in those iron-hard eyes. 'Never! I'd never have let you go without a fight, Tina! What I have I hold—and don't you ever forget it!'

'No—Paul,' she had uttered meekly, and although he wasn't really allowed to he took her in his arms and kissed her tenderly on the lips. Later in the week, on another visit, Tina quite inadvertently let slip something that her husband was quick to seize upon and she found herself being coerced into telling him of the conversation that had taken place between her and his mother. He was angry, but she coaxed him out of his anger, explaining that his mother, a Greek, had naturally expected him to marry one of his own kind, and especially as she hated the English anyway.

'I suppose you are right,' he conceded with a little sigh. 'I did in fact seriously think of marriage to Dora—'

'You led Dora to believe that you'd marry her—' Tina broke off, but it was too late. Paul was frowning, demanding to know the reason why she had said a thing like that.

'It's quite true,' he added frankly, 'but how did you come to know?'

'I had some conversation with Dora...' She had to tell him all, and again found herself coaxing him out of his anger.

'What a lot you put up with—and never said a word to me!'

'It seemed pointless, Paul.'

'Was it pointless to keep your terrible fear from me? You little idiot, Tina, likening me to a pagan who worships false gods! If I beat you when you're recovered it'll only be what you deserve.'

'But you do belong to that tribe,' she had insisted.

'It doesn't say that I follow its creed.'

'Well,' she said a trifle petulantly, 'you did frighten me on so many occasions, and each time I naturally thought of those pagans you belonged to!'

'I didn't belong to them. And if you are going to think of them when I frighten you then there's only one thing for it: I mustn't ever frighten you again.'

He was saying something of the kind when, after he had driven her home from the hospital, they sat together in the luxuriously-appointed sitting-room of the villa. It was only three weeks to Christmas now and the weather had turned cold. So a log fire had been lighted in the grate and Paul and Tina were before it, close together on a small settee.

'I never will frighten you again, my darling,' he promised, and she knew without any doubt at all that he spoke the truth.

'I'm so glad we discovered we love each other,' she murmured as with a contented little sigh she snuggled more closely into the delightful comfort of his arms. 'It took the accident to bring us together.'

'It shouldn't have done—' He broke off and she felt the strength go out of him momentarily as his body shuddered against her. 'If I'd lost you, Tina, my life would have been finished.'

Again she knew he spoke the truth. And she found herself praying that they would be together for many long years and that at the end they would go together. And somehow, she knew instinctively that her prayer would be answered.

Dusk was falling, and shadows began to encroach upon the garden and the carob slopes beyond. Through another window the sea was a wine-dark mirror spreading to where the arc of the heavens came down to meet it. So peaceful! And here inside, the pine logs burning. Tina, her heart full to overflowing, turned in her husband's arms and with a little access of love and adoration, she lifted her face, touching his lips with her own, pleading for the kiss which he was only too willing to give.